Kit suddenly found her thoughts split between what Ad was saying and the scenario forming in her head.

A scenario in which they were at the end of a date. A date she'd thoroughly enjoyed. And that they were about to kiss good-night.

But they *weren't* about to kiss good-night. "I guess I'll see you tomorrow," she forced herself to say, attempting to escape her daydream. "Thanks for all your help tonight," she said, prolonging this moment.

"Don't mention it. I'd be your kitchen assistant anytime," he joked with a lascivious note in his voice, tossing her a sexy half smile to go with it.

And that was when it struck her that Ad Walker absolutely was not like any other guy. And spending the last couple of hours with him hadn't cured whatever it was she'd been infected by the moment she'd met him.

No, if anything she thought that she really had been bitten by the Ad bug. Bitten but good.

And there was only one thing that would cure her.

Dear Reader,

Well, the lazy days of summer are winding to an end, so what better way to celebrate those last long beach afternoons than with a good book? We here at Silhouette Special Edition are always happy to oblige! We begin with *Diamonds and Deceptions* by Marie Ferrarella, the next in our continuity series, THE PARKS EMPIRE. When a mesmerizing man walks into her father's bookstore, sheltered Brooke Moss believes he's her dream come true. But he's about to challenge everything she thought she knew about her own family.

Victoria Pade continues her NORTHBRIDGE NUPTIALS with *Wedding Willies,* in which a runaway bride with an aversion to both small towns and matrimony finds herself falling for both, along with Northbridge's most eligible bachelor! In Patricia Kay's *Man of the Hour,* a woman finds her gratitude to the detective who found her missing child turning quickly to…love. In *Charlie's Angels* by Cheryl St. John, a single father is stymied when his little girl is convinced that finding a new mommy is as simple as having an angel sprinkle him with her "miracle dust"— until he meets the beautiful blonde who drives a rig called "Silver Angel." In *It Takes Three* by Teresa Southwick, a pregnant caterer sets her sights on the handsome single dad who swears his fatherhood days are behind him. Sure they are! And the MEN OF THE CHEROKEE ROSE series by Janis Reams Hudson concludes with *The Cowboy on Her Trail,* in which one night of passion with the man she's always wanted results in a baby on the way. Can marriage be far behind?

Enjoy all six of these wonderful novels, and please do come back next month for six more new selections, only from Silhouette Special Edition.

Gail Chasan
Senior Editor

Please address questions and book requests to:
Silhouette Reader Service
U.S.: 3010 Walden Ave., P.O. Box 1325, Buffalo, NY 14269
Canadian: P.O. Box 609, Fort Erie, Ont. L2A 5X3

Wedding Willies

VICTORIA PADE

Silhouette®

SPECIAL EDITION™

Published by Silhouette Books

America's Publisher of Contemporary Romance

SILHOUETTE BOOKS

ISBN 0-373-24628-5

WEDDING WILLIES

Copyright © 2004 by Victoria Pade

Books by Victoria Pade

Silhouette Special Edition

Breaking Every Rule #402
Divine Decadence #473
Shades and Shadows #502
Shelter from the Storm #527
Twice Shy #558
Something Special #600
Out on a Limb #629
The Right Time #689
Over Easy #710
Amazing Gracie #752
Hello Again #778
Unmarried with Children #852
*Cowboy's Kin #923
*Baby My Baby #946
*Cowboy's Kiss #970
Mom for Hire #1057
*Cowboy's Lady #1106

*Cowboy's Love #1159
*The Cowboy's Ideal Wife #1185
*Baby Love #1249
*Cowboy's Caress #1311
*The Cowboy's Gift-Wrapped
  Bride #1365
*Cowboy's Baby #1389
*Baby Be Mine #1431
*On Pins and Needles #1443
Willow in Bloom #1490
†*Her Baby Secret* #1503
†*Maybe My Baby* #1515
†*The Baby Surprise* #1544
His Pretend Fiancée #1564
**Babies in the Bargain #1623
**Wedding Willies #1628

*A Ranching Family
†Baby Times Three
**Northbridge Nuptials

Silhouette Books

World's Most Eligible Bachelors
Wyoming Wrangler

Montana Mavericks:
  Wed in Whitehorn
The Marriage Bargain

The Coltons
From Boss to Bridegroom

VICTORIA PADE

is a bestselling author of both historical and contemporary romance fiction, and mother of two energetic daughters, Cori and Erin. Although she enjoys her chosen career as a novelist, she occasionally laments that she has never traveled farther from her Colorado home than Disneyland, instead spending all her spare time plugging away at her computer. She takes breaks from writing by indulging in her favorite hobby—eating chocolate.

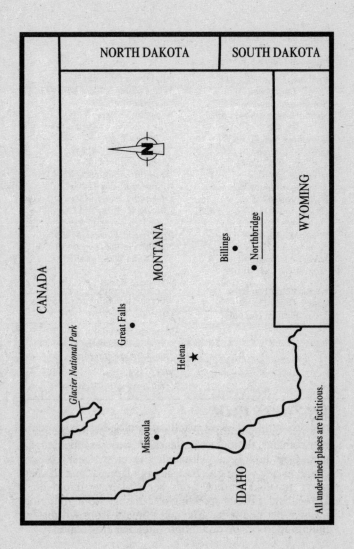

CANADA

Glacier National Park

NORTH DAKOTA

SOUTH DAKOTA

MONTANA

Great Falls

Helena ★

Missoula

Billings

● Northbridge

WYOMING

IDAHO

All underlined places are fictitious.

Chapter One

It was nearly nine-thirty on Saturday night when Kit MacIntyre's bus pulled in to Northbridge, Montana. She was the last passenger and the driver unloaded her luggage and carried it all the way into the station for her.

"I spend the night here and then do the return trip in the morning," he explained along the way.

Inside, the station was about the size of a grade-school classroom. There was no one on the pewlike benches or using the vending machines, and the elderly woman who was manning the place had already closed the ticket counter.

She greeted the driver by name, nodded to Kit, and then locked the rear door they'd come in through.

"Somebody meetin' you, sweetie?" the woman asked Kit after the driver had left through the front door.

"My friend was supposed to be here," Kit answered, scanning the space even though it was obvious there wasn't anyone else there.

"Who's your friend?" the woman inquired.

Anywhere else that question might have seemed odd, but Kit's friend had warned her that in a small town everyone knew everyone.

"Kira Wentworth," Kit informed her.

"You must be here for the wedding next Saturday," the older woman said reverently, as if the wedding were the social event of the year.

"I'm the maid of honor," Kit confirmed. "I'm also making the wedding cake."

Light seemed to dawn for the elderly woman whose blue eyes widened into saucers. "Oh, I've heard about you. My niece got married in Colorado and she wouldn't have any cake but yours—Kit's Cakes. The minute Kira told me who was making hers I recognized the name."

"That's me."

"Well, I can't wait to have that cake again. My mouth has been watering for it ever since."

"I'm glad you liked it," Kit said.

That apparently ended the cake conversation then because the woman said, "I haven't seen Kira tonight. Did she know what time the bus was getting in?"

Kit assured her that Kira did.

The woman checked the big round clock on the wall behind the ticket counter and said, "I need to close up and get home to my Henry to give him his pills. But it's a nice night. Maybe you could wait on the bench out front."

It wasn't like Kira to be unreliable so Kit felt certain her friend would be there any minute. "Would it be all right if I used the rest room first?" she asked. "I'll hurry."

"Sure thing. I'll just give my Henry a buzz and let him know I'm on my way."

Kit thanked her and followed the arrow on the aged sign that said Lavatories.

The ladies' room contained two stalls and a sink, and smelled of pine cleaner. Kit quickly entered the first stall that she came to so she could have a few minutes after she'd washed and dried her hands for a fast assessment of how she looked. She was about to meet Kira's fiancé for the first time, and she didn't want to do that all wilted and haggard.

She'd had a long day. She'd needed to put the final touches on four wedding cakes before she was able to rush home to do last-minute packing and then get to the airport. But glancing in the mirror above the sink, she decided that she wasn't too much the worse for wear.

Her pale skin needed a swipe of the blush brush from the makeup bag she took from her purse, but the mascara she'd applied that morning was still helping to darken her eyelashes. She did use her little fingers to smooth away a few smudges under her blue-violet eyes, however. Then she freshened her light mauve lipstick and pulled out the rubber band that held her hair in a ponytail.

Her hair fell to three inches below her shoulders in an

unruly cascade of curls and waves. It gave Kit fits. The curl was natural and untamable, and her hair was so thick that it always seemed too bushy to her. She'd always wished for sleek, smooth hair that she could wear in a chin-length bob, but as it was, if she cut the hair she had she lost the heaviness that helped weigh it down and ended up with what she considered clown hair.

At least she didn't mind the color, she conceded as she brushed out the dark walnut brown mass and left it to fall free around her face.

She replaced her makeup bag in her purse and left the rest room to find that it was still only the older woman waiting for her in the station.

"No Kira yet," the woman informed her.

"It's okay. I'll wait outside so you can get going," Kit assured her.

The woman led the way through the front door and Kit followed, carrying her own suitcase this time, along with the oversized shopping bag that held her pans and utensils.

Outside Kit found herself across the street from a gas station, and she spotted a pay phone she could use if Kira didn't show up soon.

As the other woman locked the door from the outside, Kit set her suitcase in front of the bench that was beside it, put her bag on the seat and sat down.

"If Kira and Cutty were still at the old house you could walk from here," the station attendant said. "The new house is farther away, though. Not too far a walk if you didn't have anything to carry, but with your suitcase and… Well, I'm sure Kira will be here any minute. I can't imagine what's keeping her."

"I'll be fine," Kit said, assuming the older woman wanted reassurance that it was okay to leave her.

She must have been right because the woman said, "I'll say good night then."

"Good night," Kit responded as the woman headed down the street on foot herself.

It was a beautiful mid-August night. Warm enough without being too hot, and there wasn't so much as a breeze to disturb the air.

But even so Kit wished that her friend would get there. It was almost eerily quiet and there wasn't a soul anywhere to be seen after the bus station attendant turned a corner about a block down.

Not that Northbridge didn't look like a nice little town from Kit's vantage point. It did. The gas station and the bus station were face-to-face at the end of Main Street, which seemed to be the gateway to the town proper.

Kit couldn't see all the way to the end of Main Street from where she was, but what she could see of it was lined on either side by two- and three-story, primarily brick structures. Quaint and old-fashioned, they had such a country-town feel to them that Kit wouldn't have been surprised to see a horse-drawn streetcar coming toward her or an old Studebaker parked at the curb somewhere along the way.

Tall, ornate wrought-iron pole lamps lit the sidewalks on both sides of the wider-than-average thoroughfare, and each light was circled with flower boxes that held the riotous yellows and oranges and burnt umbers of the marigolds planted around them.

But as nice as it looked, Kit would have preferred taking it all in on a leisurely afternoon when she and Kira could browse through the shops. At that moment she just wanted Kira to come get her.

Kit was beginning to consider crossing to the gas station to call her friend when movement quite a ways down Main Street caught her eye and distracted her.

It appeared to be a man who had just left one of the buildings, but the distance was too great for her to tell what kind of establishment he'd come out of. He was headed for her end of the street though, and despite the fact that Kit expected him to get into one of several cars parked nose-first at the curb, he just kept coming in her direction.

Maybe he would be turning off onto a side street the way the bus station woman had, Kit thought, feeling slightly edgy when that didn't seem to be happening.

She reminded herself that Kira had said Northbridge was a safe place. The man Kira was marrying was a Northbridge police officer, and he'd told Kira that keeping the peace involved mostly speeding tickets, a domestic violence complaint here and there, and underage drinking due to the presence of the small college.

But Kit felt uneasy anyway.

It was dark, after all, and she was alone without any indication that there was anyone who would hear her scream for help if she needed it. And the man not only kept coming, when he was about a block away he looked right at her, smiled and waved.

He wasn't Kira's fiancé, Kit knew that. Her friend had sent her a picture of them together, along with his twin nineteen-month-old daughters. And the man who was headed in Kit's direction was not that man.

This man was someone else.

He didn't look threatening—if that meant anything. Although he was a big son of a gun, she thought. And just because a guy was really handsome didn't mean he wasn't dangerous.

But this guy *was* really handsome. Really, really handsome. Handsome in the extreme.

Long, muscular legs were bringing him closer by the second. He had a narrow waist and broad, powerful shoulders, and he wore his sable-colored hair short on the sides and slightly longer and mussed on top. And what a face. He could have done shaving commercials with those sculpted features. High cheekbones; a wide, square forehead; a thin, almost sharp and very straight nose; lips that were a little thin but seemed to suit him just the same; and when he smiled at her yet again as he drew nearer, it put two matching creases down his cheeks and gave him a hunky, mischievous air....

"Kit?" he said when he was several yards away but close enough for her to hear him.

"Yes," she answered tentatively, not sure whether she was unsettled by being approached by a strange man on a deserted street, or by the fact that he was so amazing looking that it had sort of stunned her.

He pressed a big, long-fingered hand to the chest that was barely contained in a red knit polo shirt and said, "I'm Ad. Ad Walker. I'm a friend of Cutty's."

He said that with a question in his deep baritone voice, clearly wondering if she'd ever heard of him before.

She had. Not only had Kira talked about her fiancé's best friend, but what had prompted Kira's trip to Northbridge in search of her sister in the first place had been a newspaper article about Cutty and this man. Cutty and Addison Walker had rushed into a burning house to save the family inside. Which they'd done, only to end up injured themselves—Cutty had broken his ankle and Addison Walker had been knocked unconscious.

Not that there seemed to be any lingering effects because he looked in robust health now.

Belatedly, Kit said, "Kira told me about you. I'm Kit. Kit MacIntyre," she added, feeling foolish when she recalled that he'd already known that or he wouldn't have been able to call her by name.

Then, to make matters worse, she held out her hand with an aggressive thrust, as if she were trying to impress a prospective employer with her enthusiasm.

Ad Walker smiled and accepted her hand to shake, taking it into his massive mitt, enveloping it in a warm strength that sent heat up her arm and all through the rest of her body, and left her wondering how a mere handshake could be sensuous.

"Nice to meet you," he said.

The handshake seemed over much too quickly for Kit and she was shocked to find herself disappointed when he let go. So disappointed she had to force herself out of her own thoughts and into paying attention to what he was saying.

"Mel—one of the twins—fell and hit her head," Ad Walker explained. "Cutty and Kira had to take her in for stitches, so they asked if I'd pick you up."

"Is the baby all right?"

"She's fine. It was just a cut," he assured. "I don't know if Kira told you or not, but you'll be staying with me." He held up a big hand to wave away that last statement. "I didn't mean that the way it sounded. What I meant was, I have two apartments above my restaurant—" He poked a thumb over his shoulder in the direction from which he'd just come. "I live in one of them and I rent out the other to college kids when school is in session. But my extra apartment is vacant for the summer, and since Kira and Cutty's new house is torn up with the remodel—and since you'll be using the restaurant ovens to make the wedding cake anyway—we thought it would work out for you to use the empty apartment while you're here."

Kira *had* told Kit all that. But she liked listening to the sound of Ad Walker's voice so much that she didn't mind hearing it again.

"I hope it isn't an inconvenience for you," she said rather than letting him know he'd gone through that entire explanation for nothing.

"Nope, not at all. They're two completely separate apartments so I won't even know you're there, and you won't know I'm there, either."

Somehow Kit doubted that even separate apartments could wipe away the knowledge that this man was somewhere nearby.

But she didn't say that.

She did, however, remind herself that she was in men-pause. She was taking a hiatus from men and romance and relationships after two huge fiascoes that she took full responsibility for.

Ad Walker picked up her suitcase. "My place is just up the street. I thought we could go there, get you settled in, and then maybe get you something to eat and drink while we wait for Kira and Cutty to finish up with the baby and come by. If that's all okay with you?"

"Sounds fine." Kit took the shopping bag from the bench, explaining as she did, "I brought my own pans for the cake. I wasn't sure how equipped you were for baking."

"Beyond the ovens, I'm not equipped for baking at all," he informed her as they started off, retracing his path. "I do pub-style food—fish-and-chips, burgers, sandwiches, soups, a mean steak, ribs, barbecue, that kind of thing. The only desserts I offer are cheesecake and chocolate cake that I buy frozen from my food supplier."

"Oh dear."

Ad Walker laughed a laugh that rolled around in his chest as if it were a deep barrel. "Believe me, I'm embarrassed to admit that to someone who makes cakes for a living."

"I could teach you a few basic recipes that wouldn't

be difficult but would taste better than prepackaged, frozen, mass-produced, preservative-laden, not-much-of-a-treat desserts."

He glanced over at her, smiling. "You'd do that? Give up a couple of your world famous recipes to me?"

"Well, maybe not the *world famous* ones," she joked. "But I think I could be persuaded to teach you a few lesser-knowns for room and board this week." And she was enjoying bantering with him much more than she wanted to be.

"It's a deal," he said.

They'd reached his restaurant and bar by then.

A large neon sign proclaimed the place Adz. The front of the restaurant was mostly windows with dark green café curtains halfway up for the privacy of diners at the tables just inside. The doorway was recessed, and Ad Walker stepped into the alcove ahead of Kit to open the door for her.

The English pub theme wasn't only in the food. The dark wood paneling, dim lighting and booths that lined the walls around the freestanding tables all looked like they'd been taken straight from England or Ireland. And the long, carved, walnut bar with the brass foot rail and the full mirror behind it only added to the warm, friendly, casual ambience.

"Nice," Kit judged.

"Thanks. I like it."

Ad Walker led her through the crowd that was eating and drinking despite the fact that Kit had seen so little life on the street outside. He used his backside to push open the swinging doors to one side of the bar and waited for Kit to precede him into the kitchen.

The kitchen was impressively clean and much the same as most restaurant kitchens—a brightly lit space with sinks and stoves and ovens lining the walls, and workstations in the form of stainless steel tables in the center.

Ad wasn't paid a lot of attention by the staff, who were busy with their own duties, as he took Kit to the rear door and out into an alley.

It was a very appealing alley, though. The street was brick-paved to make it look cobbled, the buildings were all painted, windows were shuttered, trash receptacles were enclosed and carriage lights provided illumination from both sides.

"We're up here," Ad said, nodding to the wooden staircase that ran alongside the restaurant's back wall to a wide, railed landing that accommodated two doors.

Ad unlocked the first door they came to and then gave Kit the key that he'd used. Once she'd accepted it he reached in, turned on a light and waited for her to precede him inside.

Kit did, finding a small studio apartment complete with a double bed and dresser in one section; a tiny kitchenette in another; and a sofa, matching chair, a desk and a television in another section.

"The place is kind of bare-bones," Ad said apologetically. Then he stretched out a long arm and pointed at the two doors at the opposite end of the apartment. "Left is closet, right is bathroom. I put clean sheets on the bed this morning, fresh towels are in the linen cupboard in the bath. The fridge is stocked with a few essentials but not many, and there's no coffee or coffeepot, but whatever you want to eat or drink is yours for the asking from the restaurant."

He was right, the furniture was sparse and unassuming, but the place was neat and tidy and dust-free, the walls looked newly whitewashed, and all in all it seemed comfortable.

"I don't expect you to feed me the whole time I'm here but the apartment will do just fine. In fact, it's cozy. I like it," Kit assured him, meaning it.

He lifted her suitcase over the brass footboard that matched the bed's brass headboard and set it on the mattress as Kit put the shopping bag on the tiny kitchen table.

They turned to face each other at about the same time and that was when Kit was treated to the sight of his eyes.

The man had amazing, vibrant, bright aquamarine-colored eyes.

And for a moment she got lost in them.

Until his deep voice brought her out of it.

"So, do you want some time up here alone or shall we just go down and get you fed?"

Since she'd already used the rest room at the bus station, she said, "To tell you the truth I didn't have time to eat all day and I'm starved. I think I'll just take you up on dinner."

He smiled as if that was what he'd been hoping to

hear, putting those intriguing creases down the sides of his handsome face. "Great. Let's go."

They hadn't closed the door and this time Ad stepped outside ahead of her, as if giving the place over to her as her own.

Kit followed him out, flipping off the wall switch beside the door to turn off the overhead lights he'd turned on before. Then she checked to make sure the door was locked and closed it after herself.

"I recommend the fish-and-chips. They're especially good tonight," Ad said as they retraced their path down the stairs. "But you can have whatever you want."

"Fish-and-chips it is. And iced tea if you have it."

They went back in through the kitchen and Ad told the cook they needed an order of fish-and-chips sent out. Then he took her into the restaurant once more.

He poured two glasses of iced tea from a pitcher behind the bar before nodding to a small corner table that was free.

"Let's sit over there," he suggested.

"Don't feel as if you have to keep me company if there's something else you need—or want—to do," Kit felt obliged to say.

"There isn't anything else I need—or want—to do," he answered, making her wonder if there had been special emphasis on the *or want* part, or if she'd just been imagining it.

Then, as if it had just occurred to him that she might not want his company, he said, "Unless *you'd* rather be alone—"

"No," Kit answered much too quickly. "I just don't want to be a bother."

"It's no bother. I've been kind of enjoying myself," he said.

That pleased her more than it should have but Kit tried to ignore it and made her way to the table.

They settled in across from each other and as Kit took a sip of her tea she worked to come up with something to talk about with this man she'd just met…and couldn't seem to keep her eyes off of.

But then she doubted it would be easy for any normal, red-blooded woman not to look at that handsome face and the muscular body that went with it.

It was that robustly healthy physique that suddenly spurred the memory of the newspaper article that had been her first exposure to Ad Walker and she seized that to make conversation with.

"I heard about you and Cutty saving that family from their burning house and about you both getting hurt. How are you after getting beamed?"

Ad smiled. "Shouldn't that be *beaned?*"

"As I recall you didn't get hit with a *bean,* you got hit with a *beam,*" she said, smiling to let him know her play on words had been just that.

"I'm as good as new." He tapped on his head as if knocking on a door. "Hard head."

"Not hard enough to keep you out of the hospital for a couple of days—or so I heard."

"I'm okay now, though. But thanks for asking."

"Kira said Cutty got the cast off his ankle last week

and he's doing all right, too," Kit said, trying to keep things going.

"He did. And the burned house has been repaired, and the family we dragged out of it has moved back in, and even the dog's singed tail looks normal again. It's as if it all never happened."

"Except that as a result of it I no longer have my best friend living across the hall from me," Kit pointed out as a waitress served her meal.

When she'd thanked the woman, Kit shot another sly smile in Ad's direction and added, "Of course I blame you for that."

Ad laughed. "Me? What did I do?"

"You talked to Kira about Cutty and that was instrumental in her decision to pursue her relationship with him."

"Ah." Ad's engaging grin said that he realized she was only teasing him. But rather than commenting on the subject of the part he'd played in his friend's romance, he nodded at her plate with his chin. "How's your food?" he asked.

Kit had tasted both the beer-battered, deep-fried cod and the French fries and could honestly say, "It's the best fish-and-chips I've ever had. But don't think it makes up for costing me my best friend."

"Doesn't it make up for it a little?"

Was he flirting with her?

Had she been flirting with him?

Kit wasn't sure on either count. But she was enjoying the exchange just the same.

"It makes up for it very little," she countered.

"Hmm. Well, as I understand it, you did some encouraging of your own when it came to the fork in the road for Kira and Cutty. Kira told me you opened her eyes to some things that got her to thinking and ultimately coming back here to Cutty."

"It was already too late by the time I got in on this. I just had to roll with things," Kit claimed. "So I still blame you."

Okay, maybe that *had* sounded slightly flirtatious. *Stop it!* she told herself.

"I guess I'll have to think of a way to make it up to you," Ad conceded with an innuendo-laden tone of his own.

Kit played along with skepticism. "That's a tall order."

"I love a challenge," he said.

His aquamarine eyes glinted with mischief and held hers in a spell that left Kit completely unaware of anything or anyone else around them.

So completely unaware that she only realized her friend was standing right beside the table when she heard, "Umm, are we interrupting something?"

Ad seemed as surprised as Kit felt to discover that Kira Wentworth and Cutty Grant had joined them.

"Kira!" Kit exclaimed, jumping to her feet to cover her own preoccupation with a man she had no business being preoccupied with.

Kira gave her a hug and said, "I'm so sorry I couldn't meet your bus! I made you come all the way to Montana, and I wasn't even there when you got here. But

Mel fell against the corner of the fireplace in the new house and cut her forehead. We had to take her in for stitches."

"I know, Ad told me. It's okay," Kit said.

But Kira went on anyway. "I couldn't leave her. She was scared and upset and she doesn't like anything to do with doctors as it is, let alone having to get three stitches, poor thing. And then we decided that rather than push it, we should just get the girls home and put them to bed and call the sitter to stay with them after we got them to sleep for the night."

"I totally understand. You needed to do what was best for the babies. Really, it was no big deal. I'm just glad to see you now," Kit assured.

Ad had risen to his feet when Kit had and he'd been very busy pulling two chairs from another table.

"What can I get you guys?" he asked then. "Something to eat? To drink?"

"I'll have a beer," Cutty said.

"Nothing for me," this from Kira. "I just want Kit to meet Cutty."

While Ad got Cutty's beer Kira introduced Kit and Cutty and by the time that was accomplished and the four of them were situated around the small table whatever it was that had been going on between Kit and Ad Walker before Kira's and Cutty's appearance had been put to an end.

But as happy as Kit was to see her best friend and to meet the man who had made Kira nearly glow with delight, as happy as Kit was to know that their baby daughter was okay, there was still a tiny speck of regret lurking deep down in her.

A spark of regret that had something to do with Ad Walker.

And with that interruption of whatever it was that had been going on between them.

Chapter Two

After a night of tossing and turning, Ad was up early Sunday morning. Not only was he up, he was in the kitchen of his apartment rushing to fix a big breakfast, keeping a vigilant eye out the window over the sink that afforded him a view of the alley—and the landing he shared with Kit—and silently berating himself for all of it.

The tossing and turning hadn't been simply an ordinary restless night. He hadn't been up since the crack of dawn just because he was an early riser. The breakfast he was making was double what he could eat and he wasn't in a hurry because he was hungry. And he wasn't watching the weather change through that window.

Kit MacIntyre—she was the reason for everything.

He'd had a bad night's sleep because he hadn't been able to get her out of his head, and dreaming about her had woken him up before his alarm had gone off in the morning.

He was making double the food so he would have an excuse to invite her to breakfast.

He was hurrying to do it and keeping an eye out for her to make sure she didn't go down to the restaurant before he had the chance to convince her to come to his place instead.

And those were all absolutely the *wrong* reasons for everything. He just couldn't seem to help himself.

But then it wasn't every day that he met someone he hit it off with the way he'd hit it off with Kit. Someone he felt so comfortable with. Someone who—unless he was mistaken—had been pretty relaxed with him, too.

Conversation hadn't been a struggle. They'd fallen easily into teasing each other. Into joking around. Their whole time together had been... Well, fun. It was as simple as that.

But simple or not, that hadn't happened for him in a long while.

Oh, sure, it was easy enough to talk to other women he knew. To tease them and joke around with them. But last night, with Kit, there had been an added element to it. A different dynamic.

Attraction.

Okay, he admitted it. He'd felt an attraction to Kit. Much as he didn't want to. And he *didn't* want to.

What had he sworn to himself after Lynda?

No out-of-towners.

It wasn't a difficult concept. He didn't want to get involved with any woman who had a life and ties outside Northbridge. Certainly no one who had a whole business somewhere else.

So what the hell was he doing? he asked himself as he began to scramble eggs.

He took another peek out the window in the direction of the studio apartment. That simple gesture was enough to put the picture of Kit into his head even though there was no sign of her.

It was a phenomena that had been happening since she'd left him in the restaurant the night before. Every detail of the way Kit looked would pop into his head even when he was trying not to think about her or trying to talk himself out of the things she'd roused in him. Out of the blue the image of her would invade in bright, living color. And it certainly wasn't helping anything.

How could it when he liked the way she looked so damn much?

That was somewhat of a puzzler all on its own.

He usually went for the surfer-girl types—sleek, sun-streaked blond hair; healthy tans that spoke of athletic, outdoorsy interests; long legs that went on forever.

And that wasn't Kit.

Kit had crazy-wild espresso-colored hair that made her look a little untamed. And it framed pale, flawless, alabaster skin that didn't seem to have ever seen the unblocked sun. Plus she wasn't particularly leggy. How could she be when she was barely more than three or four inches over five feet tall?

But still it all worked for her.

He didn't think he'd ever seen anyone with features that fine and delicate. With cheekbones that high. With a nose that thin and impeccably shaped. With lips that were a perfect mix of full and pink and perfect. With dark, purplish blue eyes.

Violet—that's what they were. The color of the flowers on that bush his mother loved so much. Blue-violet eyes. Big, round, sparkling blue-violet eyes with the longest, thickest black lashes....

Ad sighed a long sigh.

She also had a terrific little body. Tight and compact with breasts that had drawn his attention and thoughts more than once, and a rear end that would just fit in his hands....

Yeah. He definitely liked the way she looked.

But she lives in Denver, he reminded himself. *She has a business in Denver. She's only here until after the wedding.*

That reminder was supposed to be the antidote.

But all it had accomplished was to leave him thinking about how he had the whole week with Kit right next door.

"You're just asking for misery," he muttered in warning. The kind of misery he'd suffered before. The kind of misery he was determined not to ever suffer again.

So he knew that what he should do was eat this breakfast by himself, not see Kit any more than necessary while she was here, and squelch the hell out of that mental picture of her that kept raising things he didn't want raised.

No doubt about it, that's what he should do.

Except that just then he heard the door on the studio apartment open and close.

And did he do what he *should* do? Did he ignore it and count himself lucky not to have to see her first thing this morning?

No, he didn't.

He dropped everything to charge to his own door and fling it open before any better judgment had a chance to take hold.

"Oh, you scared me," Kit said, pressing a hand to her chest.

"I'm sorry," he apologized.

She had on a pair of white short-shorts that made him think twice about the notion that she didn't have long legs, and a red cap-sleeved T-shirt that fit tight enough to give him pause. And her hair was a loose cascade of curls and waves, and she looked all fresh-scrubbed and...

And wow!

It took him a moment to remember what he was doing and get back on track.

"I wanted to catch you before you hit the restaurant for breakfast," he explained. "I thought maybe you'd like to share mine."

"That's nice," she said, making him realize just then that he even liked the sound of her voice—a soft, sexy voice that went on to say, "Kira called a little while ago and said she'd be here to pick me up earlier than we planned last night. I'm going down to meet her now. Thanks, though."

"Sure. Anytime," Ad answered as if it didn't matter

to him one way or another. Which was how it was sup-posed to be. But wasn't.

"Does the restaurant close early tonight since it's Sunday?" she asked then.

"Yeah, at eight."

"I was thinking that if that was the case maybe to-night would be a good night for me to bake the cakes. I always do them ahead anyway and freeze them, and if the kitchen will be free—"

"Tonight would be good," Ad assured her. "I hadn't thought about it, but you're right, with the place closed you can have free rein."

She seemed to hesitate slightly before she said, "I was also thinking that—if it wouldn't be a huge hassle for you and you don't have other plans—it might help if you're there."

"You want me to play assistant pastry chef?"

"No, but you could point out where the bowls and utensils are, how to work your mixer, how long your oven takes to preheat, if there are any hot spots—things like that. I just don't know the workings of your kitchen."

"Sure. No problem," he said as if he wasn't already looking forward to being alone with her.

"You don't have other plans?" she asked.

"Tallying up weekend receipts—but I think they can wait."

"You don't mind?"

"Nope."

"Great. I'll see you tonight, after eight, then."

"I'll be here."

Horn dog. You're just a damn horn dog, Walker, he chastised himself.

Kit headed down the stairs then and Ad's eyes went with her, riding the small swell of the pockets of her shorts and sliding along the backs of smooth thighs and trim calves all the way to thin ankles and bare feet cushioned by a pair of sandals that exposed painted toenails.

"Have a nice day in the meantime," she called to him.

"You, too," he responded in a voice that was huskier than it should have been.

Denver. She lives in Denver. Remember Lynda and that year and after that year...

But nothing did the trick.

Ad was still looking forward to tonight. After eight...

Standing in front of Ad's restaurant waiting for Kira to pick her up, Kit felt more self-conscious than she had since she was a gawky teenager in high school.

What had she been thinking to wear these shorts? she demanded of herself.

She'd bought them on a whim, without trying them on, and then brought them home to realize when she did slip into them that there was no way she was ever going to wear them. They were just *too* short.

But she hadn't paid a lot for them and she also hadn't had the time to return them, so she'd packed them to bring to Northbridge with her, thinking that maybe the teenage baby-sitter Kira referred to frequently would like them.

Yet there Kit was, wearing those shorts herself.

And feeling really stupid in them.

And even more stupid for *why* she was in them.

She'd brought perfectly nice clothes with her. Perfectly sensible, tasteful clothes. Clothes that she looked good in and felt comfortable wearing.

But when she'd surveyed them this morning to choose an outfit for today they'd all seemed so lifeless, so dull, so ordinary.

Not that the clothes had changed. It was just that she'd been under the influence.

No, she hadn't been drinking mimosas for breakfast or anything. She'd been under the influence of Ad Walker.

Of course he had no idea he was having any effect on her. But still he'd influenced her choice because it had been with him in mind that she'd opted for these dumb shorts. With him in mind and with the overwhelming desire to have his eyes pop right out of their sockets when he saw her.

And she just wanted to kick herself for it.

Yes, she'd enjoyed the reaction she'd gotten when he'd seen her a few minutes earlier. She'd even liked that his voice had suddenly gotten huskier.

But honestly, what was the point? It wasn't as if she wanted to start anything with Ad. It wasn't as if she should care whether or not he noticed her at all.

He was just a guy. The best friend of her best friend's fiancé. They were going to be in a wedding together. They would see each other off and on this week in connection with that, and then they would go their separate ways.

So why did having him notice her, having him like what he was seeing, feel like such a big deal to her?

And that wasn't the only question she asked herself. There were more to go with that one.

Like, why had he been on her mind almost since the minute she'd set eyes on him? And why had she gone to bed last night wondering where on the other side of their shared wall he might be sleeping himself? And in what? And why had he been the first thing she'd thought about when she'd woken up this morning?

Okay, she reasoned, she'd met an attractive man—a man so *powerfully* attractive that he'd canceled out her better judgment and the lessons she *had* learned, and caused her to backslide.

But that didn't mean that it had to go any farther than giving in to the impulse to wear these shorts.

She just wouldn't let anything else like this happen from here on. As soon as she got to Kira's house she would borrow something from her friend, take off the shorts and get rid of them forever. And she would make sure that she kept everything—including Ad Walker— in perspective.

She was only in Northbridge for this week. And Ad Walker was nothing more than one of several members of the wedding party. Someone she needed to be polite and cordial to, and nothing more.

So what if he had incredible aquamarine eyes, and a chiseled chin, and a body that was big and muscular and irresistible enough to weaken women's knees from coast to coast?

So what if her knees felt a little weak just picturing him in her mind? So what if her pulse picked up a little speed at the thought that she was going to get to spend some time alone with him tonight?

Where she could sneak peeks at that fabulous derriere of his. And hear his voice. And his laugh. And make him smile so she could see those deep dimples that creased his cheeks when he did....

Maybe she should keep the shorts on...

No! No! No! she silently shrieked at herself when she realized where her thoughts had wandered. *Again.*

She had to stop doing that. She had to stop drifting off into those mini-daydreams and fantasies of Ad Walker. She had to keep her focus on the wedding, on Kira. She had to remember that when it came to men— no matter how handsome or personable or sexy or interesting or funny or fun—she had to pass. She had to. She'd made the decision to suspend her men-privileges for good reason and she intended to stick to it.

No matter how difficult sticking to her guns might be with a man like Ad Walker right under her nose.

Just then a station wagon pulled up to the curb in front of her. Kira was behind the wheel, and Kit nearly leaped into the passenger seat when the car stopped.

"I need to borrow some more conservative shorts or some jeans or something," she announced without even saying hello.

"Okay," Kira said, sounding confused.

"This is the first time I've had these on and I don't like them."

"They are pretty short," Kira agreed. "But I can wait while you go up and change if you want. There's no hurry."

There might not be any hurry but if Kit went back upstairs to change that would mean she might run into Ad. And if she ran into Ad she might have to explain what she was doing. And he might realize she'd temporarily lost her mind. Over him.

But rather than saying any of that to Kira, Kit said, "I hate to go all the way through the restaurant. I'll just wear something of yours and you can see if your baby-sitter wants these. I'll need a rubber band to put my hair up, too. I shouldn't have left it down today. It'll drive me crazy."

"Okay," Kira repeated. "Are you all right?"

Apparently either what Kit had said or the fact that she sounded desperate spurred her friend's concern or curiosity.

"Just uncomfortable in these shorts," Kit lied.

Uncomfortable in the shorts and in her skin and with just being in the same town Ad Walker was in.

"Okay," Kira said a third time, still with a query in her voice.

But at least she put the car into motion and drove Kit away from the general proximity of Ad Walker.

Unfortunately for Kit, though, even distance from the man didn't dilute her response to him or the fact that she was going to be seeing him again that evening.

Which brought a tiny tingle of excitement at the prospect.

Excitement she knew she should absolutely not be feeling.

Under ordinary circumstances she would have confided in Kira everything she was thinking—and doing—in regard to Ad Walker. They would have talked about it all, laughed about it, aired it out, and she would likely have felt better. Kira would also likely have put it into perspective, which would have helped Kit understand what was going on and that might have allowed her to beat into submission the fledgling, unwanted attraction to him.

But despite spending all day and through dinner that evening with Kira, Kit didn't get the opportunity to talk to her best friend privately.

During the ten-minute drive to Kira and Cutty's new house, Kira laid out a hectic schedule for that day and for the rest of this last week before the wedding. And when they reached the two-story colonial that Kira and Cutty and the twins had moved into, it was a beehive of activity and commotion.

Cutty was there trying to look after the busy nineteen-month-old babies who were into everything. There were plumbers who were remodeling one of the bathrooms, and there was also an elderly woman named Betty to help Kit and Kira make little bundles of nuts and candy for each place setting at the reception tables.

Betty had been Cutty's housekeeper and nanny before Kira's appearance in his life, and had initially been a source of trouble for Kira. But now that Kira and Cutty were marrying, Betty only helped out with the twins and the house on a part-time basis, and she and Kira had become friends.

With so many people around and so much to do, Kit never found a minute to tell her friend that she was having problems keeping Ad Walker off her mind.

And then the day was over and on the drive back to the restaurant Kira outlined what needed to be done the next day, not giving Kit the chance to tell her anything before dropping her off in the alley at the foot of the steps that led up to the apartments.

So Kit was on her own.

And facing an evening of baking cakes in Ad's restaurant kitchen…with the delectable Ad.

She went upstairs to the studio apartment, slipping inside without seeing the man who, even throughout the well-occupied day, had haunted her.

But maybe, she began to think as she closed the door behind her, she'd just built this out of proportion in her mind. She hadn't spent a whole lot of time with him, she reasoned. And she'd been traveling and was tired. Really tired. Everything might have combined to skew her image of Ad Walker. To make him seem better than he really was.

And then maybe her imagination had just kept it going. Expanded on it. And maybe the end result was that Ad Walker had seemed more fantastic than he actually was.

Although he *had* looked good when she'd seen him for those few minutes this morning….

But now that she was rested, she expected to see that he honestly was just a guy like any other guy. That he wasn't anything special. And then she would be cured of whatever she'd been infected by.

She was convinced of it.

Feeling more equipped to see him again, Kit set about getting ready.

She'd borrowed a pair of shorts from Kira but decided that her legs should be covered completely before she encountered Ad again. The less skin that showed, the better. So she slipped out of them and into a pair of jeans.

The chef's coat she'd brought with her provided coverage of the red T-shirt, and she put it on over both jeans and shirt, telling herself that it was good that she looked boxy and sexless in it.

She left her hair trussed up on the crown of her head in the rubber band she'd taken from Kira, but she did give in to the inclination to refresh her blush and mascara—telling herself it was harmless.

Once she'd done that, she took the shopping bag containing her bakeware, utensils and some ingredients, and went back down the steps.

He's just a guy like any other guy, she repeated to herself along the way. *He's not anything special. He's just a regular guy.*

A regular guy who would probably run screaming into the night if he knew her track record.

With her hand on the alley door to the kitchen, Kit braced herself, determined that she would take being with Ad in stride.

And that was exactly what she intended.

But intentions aside, the minute she opened that door and went in, she couldn't help eagerly scanning the place for him.

Anymore than she could help the wave of instant disappointment when she discovered that the kitchen was empty.

Or the utter elation when, a moment later, he came through the swinging doors that connected the dining room to the kitchen.

"There you are," he greeted when he spotted her. "I was beginning to wonder if you'd forgotten about me."

I wish I could.... "I wanted to make sure your customers were all gone and your staff had finished up for the night before I barged in," she lied, rather than let him know eight o'clock had come and gone while she'd been trying to get herself in the right frame of mind to see him again.

One look at him shot a hole through the theory that he was just a regular guy, though. The man was staggeringly handsome and that fact struck Kit all over again.

He had on a simple pair of jeans and a hunter-green polo shirt with the restaurant's name embroidered above the breast pocket. But both the jeans and the shirt fit him to perfection, accentuating broad shoulders and chest, narrow waist and hips and thick thighs.

Plus he appeared to have taken the time to shave very recently and he smelled terrific, too—a clean, sea-breeze scent that was tantalizing and seductive and...

And she needed to get her head out of the clouds!

"How about a glass of iced tea or lemonade while we work?" Ad offered.

"Lemonade sounds good," Kit accepted, wondering if she should just pour the cold liquid over her head.

While Ad filled two glasses she forced herself to get busy so she wasn't just standing there gawking at him.

She went to the stainless steel work table in the center of the room and began to unload her things from the giant-sized shopping bag.

"I brought my own sugar, flour, vanilla and liqueur because they aren't the everyday varieties. I also had Kira get the grocery store here to order in the European butter I use, but she said you'd told her I could steal the eggs from you," Kit chattered to conceal her reaction to him.

"Yeah, I think I can spare a few eggs," he confirmed. "And anything else you might need."

"I shouldn't need anything else. Except raspberries and cream later. But I can pick up those when the time comes. Oh, and chocolate," Kit added when she reached it at the bottom of the bag. "I also brought my own chocolate—white and bittersweet. They have to be a certain kind, too."

Ad brought the glasses of lemonade to the worktable and handed one of them to Kit. "Raspberries and chocolate? I take it you aren't doing a run-of-the-mill cake."

Kit sipped her drink, peering over the rim of the glass at the oh-so-yummy man with the aquamarine eyes. "I'm making a dark chocolate cake that I'll brush with a raspberry liqueur called framboise," she explained. "Then, on each cake, there will be a layer of chocolate ganache, then a layer of thickened fresh raspberry puree. I'll cover all that in a thin frosting of the chocolate ganache, then do a second frosting and the decorations in white-chocolate butter cream."

"Holy cow. Better make a big cake, people around Northbridge don't see anything as fancy as that. I can guarantee they'll go back for seconds."

"I'm making four graduated tiers with five satellite cakes around the bottom tier. Kira wants to be sure there's plenty."

Ad counted the variously sized round cake pans Kit had stacked on the table.

"Yep, nine pans. Looks like we have our work cut out for us." He held his arms wide. "Use me as you will."

Kit laughed and tried not to think of better uses for him than buttering and flouring pans.

But that was the task she gave him—along with cutting rounds of parchment paper for the bottoms of each one.

While Ad did that Kit began beating egg whites and putting the cake batter together.

With the electric mixer running the noise level was too high for them to talk much. Mostly Kit gave instructions and Ad did as he was told. It might have been better if they *had* been able to keep up a conversation because maybe then it wouldn't have been so difficult for Kit to keep from sneaking peeks at him, from noticing how adept his hands were, how agile his long, thick fingers could be. It might not have been so difficult to keep from studying the furrows his brow creased into as he concentrated on what he was doing. It might not have been so difficult to keep from glancing in the direction of his derriere when he dropped the scissors and bent over to retrieve them.

When the cakes were in the ovens, Kit and Ad

worked together on the cleanup. Once that was accomplished they were left with nothing to do but wait.

"Let's sit out where it's cooler," Ad suggested, nodding toward the front half of the restaurant.

They left the swinging doors open so Kit could hear the timer on the ovens, taking refills of lemonade with them.

Chairs were up on the tables in the seating area but Ad took two down for them to sit. Without thinking about it, Kit did what she would have done at any other time after finishing her baking—she took off her chef's coat.

Only after she had did she recall that she'd been using it not only as protection from splatters, but also as camouflage for the tight red T-shirt she'd put on that morning with Ad in mind.

But it was too late to cover up again and she just pretended not to notice how his eyes dropped momentarily to her breasts in an appreciative glance that she found much too gratifying.

"So, you seem to know your way around a restaurant kitchen," he said after they'd each taken a seat at the table.

"I should. My first job was making pizzas in my Uncle Mackie's bar. Uncle Mackie was my mother's brother. He had a little neighborhood place around the corner from the house where I grew up."

Ad seemed to find pleasure in that information because he smiled. "You were a pizza-maker?" he said as if he didn't believe it.

"I could throw the dough in the air and catch it and everything," she bragged with a laugh.

"I'd like to see that sometime," he said, quirking up his left eyebrow to make the comment seem lascivious.

"I'll bet you would," she countered.

"Is pizza-making what got you interested in baking?" he asked then.

"I'd always liked making cookies as a kid, but—as a matter of fact—it *was* the pizza-making that started the wheels turning for me as a baker. I loved the feel of the dough. The smell of the yeast. Being able to turn a few simple ingredients into something mouthwatering."

Now *she* was giving a sensual tone to it all.

She consciously curbed it.

"Anyway," she continued, "I started to experiment with adding more sugar to the pizza dough so I could make cinnamon rolls. I went from those to quick breads, then cakes and more complicated cookies than I'd made as a kid. Pies and tarts and tortes came next, and by the time I graduated from high school I knew I wanted to go to culinary school rather than college and be a pastry chef."

"Did you stay at your uncle's bar all the way through that?"

"I did. And for a while even after I graduated. He gave me part of his kitchen to work in and featured any kind of dessert I wanted to make. Where else could I go and do exactly as I pleased fresh out of school?"

"When *did* you leave your uncle's place then?"

"When I wanted to start my own bakery. I spent two years after school saving every penny until I had enough to rent the storefront next to the bar and buy the ovens and equipment I needed."

"Do you still work out of that storefront?"

"No," Kit said after a drink of lemonade. "I stayed there for a few years but the business grew and I needed more space. By then I also realized I was making most of my money from the cakes, so I changed from a bakery that offered breads, rolls and other pastries to Kit's Cakes."

"Which, according to what I've heard, took off. It's hard to believe you can make a living just doing wedding cakes."

Kit laughed at his skepticism. "I do other cakes, too. For parties, retirement send-offs, graduations, wedding and baby showers, birthdays. But, yes, most of my living comes from the wedding cakes. I'm doing Kira and Cutty's cake as part of their present, but you'd be surprised what I can charge for it. Let's hope getting married never goes out of style," Kit finished with a joke that made him smile again and dimple up for her.

The timer rang, and without saying anything, Kit hurried into the kitchen. She didn't expect Ad to follow her but he did, expressing an interest in how she knew when the cakes were done.

She demonstrated the method of using a cake tester and then pressed a gentle finger to the center of one cake to show him what he should be looking for that way, too. In case he actually did ever bake the recipe she'd promised him.

The cakes were sufficiently baked but she explained that they couldn't be removed from the pans for ten minutes. Then they had to be completely cooled in order to wrap them and store them in the freezer.

When the ten minutes had passed she flipped the cakes and removed the circles of parchment paper that had come out with the rich chocolate confection. Then she and Ad washed the pans before returning to the dining room to sit again.

"If you're bored or have something else to do I can take it from here," Kit told him, realizing belatedly that there wasn't much reason for him to stay at that point.

"I'm not bored and there's nothing I'd rather be doing," he assured, pleasing her more than she wanted to show.

"Okay. Then what about you?" she asked after more lemonade. "How did you get into the bar and restaurant business?"

"I started busing tables here," he said with an affectionate glance around. "When I was ten."

"Ten?" Kit parroted. "Wasn't that a little on the young side? Like by about six years?"

"My dad was a mechanic and when I was ten a car he was working under fell on him. He was killed—"

"Oh, I'm so sorry," Kit said, flinching at the image.

"It was a long time ago. But my mom hadn't held a job before that and was left with five small kids to support on only a pittance for an insurance policy. She went to work at the dry cleaners but we were still struggling and—in my ten-year-old brain—I thought I could help."

Kit pictured Ad as a boy who felt that kind of responsibility, and she was torn between her heart breaking for him and admiring how at even that young age he'd taken action to help his family.

"How did you get hired when you were hardly more than a baby?" she asked.

"Bing—Bingham Murphy—owned the place then and he sponsored and coached our little league baseball team. He was always saying he needed help sweeping the floors or taking out the trash if somebody wanted to earn a little money for a new bike or something. It wasn't really like being *hired,* it was more like getting an allowance for doing chores. But when I talked to Bing and told him what was going on at home, he let it be my job exclusively from then on."

"Did you work every day? After school? Weekends?"

"After school or after baseball practice and on weekends. I'd sweep floors and the sidewalk out front. Wash windows. Take out the trash. Bus the tables. Pour water for customers. Small stuff."

"And this Bing-person would pay you?"

"Right. Plus, folks around here knew us and knew what had happened to my Dad and wanted to help without it seeming like charity, so they'd tip me. It added up. I didn't do too bad."

"For a ten-year-old."

"Hey, I ended up owning the place," he joked as if his childhood earnings had accomplished that.

"How *did* you end up owning the place?" Kit asked.

"Stick-to-ittiveness. I stayed put, moved up from busboy to doing just about everything else there was to do—wait tables, tend bar, cook. By the time I was working my way through the local college for my business degree, Bing had retired and I was running things. Then he offered to sell out to me and I made payments to him until it was all mine—the business and the building. Two years ago I renovated and remodeled until it really felt like my own place."

"So you found your niche at ten years old?" Kit summarized.

"That's really the truth. I always liked being here. I liked the work, the socializing. I just felt right at home from the start."

"I understand that. I felt that way at my uncle's place. It was hard work but it was nice."

And so was sitting there like that, with Ad, having an excuse to look at him, to get to know the intricacies of his features, the way his eyes could actually go from aquamarine to dark turquoise with the changes in his emotions....

But letting herself be mesmerized by it all was not wise, and Kit knew it.

It just wasn't a breeze to tear herself away.

She did it, though, standing up and taking her glass with her.

"Those cakes should be cool enough by now."

Ad stood, too, following her back to the kitchen.

He played assistant again as she wrapped the cooled cakes in plastic and then sealed them in bags and stored them in the walk-in freezer where they would be left undisturbed by his staff.

Then Kit gathered her equipment, Ad turned off the

lights, and they went out the alley door, locking it behind them.

The whole way up the stairs Kit had to fight feeling sad that her time with Ad was ending but she did that, too, reminding herself that this was a temporary, superficial relationship and not the beginning of something. Even if it did *feel* like the beginning of something.

"Did Kira tell you that we have fittings on the wedding clothes tomorrow afternoon?" Ad asked when they reached the landing of the side-by-side doors to the two apartments.

"She did," Kit confirmed, trying not to breathe too deeply of the scent of his cologne because either that or just being so near to him was making her head go a tiny bit woozy.

"The tailor is just up the street, how about if we walk over together?" he suggested.

That pleased her way, *way,* too much.

"Okay," she said as if it didn't make any difference.

"I thought maybe afterward we could have dinner back here—Kira and Cutty and you and me. Since they'll already have Betty staying with the twins and I know they're both tired and stressed out dealing with the wedding and the construction on the house, dinner out might be a little break for them."

"I think it might," Kit agreed.

He nodded toward his door. "I'll go in and call Cutty right now to make the arrangements."

"Good idea."

But he didn't do that. Instead he glanced over her

head at her door and said, "Did you do all right in the apartment last night? You had everything you needed? The bed wasn't too hard or too soft?"

"I did great, had everything I needed and the bed was perfect." Except that she'd had trouble not thinking about him in his bed next door.

"So you're okay over there?"

"Fine," she said, wondering if she was imagining it or whether he was purposely dragging this out.

Not that she was rushing inside herself. In fact she wasn't even altogether invested in what they were talking about because even though she was making all the right responses to what he was saying, Kit was suddenly finding her thoughts split between that and a scenario that was forming in her head.

A scenario in which they were at the end of a date.

A date she'd enjoyed.

And they were about to kiss good-night.

But they *weren't* about to kiss good-night.

"I guess I'll see you tomorrow," she forced herself to say, attempting to escape her daydream.

Ad nodded, but he continued to look at her as if he were trying to read something in her eyes.

A moment of panic ran through Kit at the notion that he could somehow tell what she'd been thinking.

But then Ad finally took the last step to his own door and said, "Good night."

"Thanks for the use of your kitchen and all your help tonight," she added as she unlocked and opened her door, doing a little prolonging of her own.

"Don't mention it. I'd be your assistant anytime," he joked with another lascivious note in his voice, tossing her a sexy half-smile to go with it.

"Careful, I might take you up on that," she warned as she stepped into the studio apartment and closed the door behind her.

And that was when it struck her again that Ad Walker absolutely was not like any other guy.

And that spending the last couple of hours with him hadn't cured whatever it was she'd been infected by the moment she'd met him.

No, if anything she thought that she really had been bitten by the Ad bug. Bitten but good.

And she wasn't sure what to do about it….

Chapter Three

"Oh, Kira, it's even more beautiful than I pictured from your description," Kit told her friend late Monday when she got her first glimpse of Kira in her wedding dress.

After another long day of dealing with last-minute R.S.V.P.s, the caterer and seating arrangements, it was after five o'clock before Kira and Kit had been able to leave Betty with the twins and get to the tailor's shop for the final fittings on their dresses. The delay had necessitated Kira calling both Cutty and Ad to tell them to go on their own for the alterations of their tuxedos and that they could all meet up later at the restaurant for dinner.

There hadn't been anything Kit could do about it, but she'd regretted that she and Ad hadn't been able to have that walk to the shop together the way they'd planned.

"It's just beautiful," she repeated as Kira stepped up

onto the raised platform in the center of the open room where the tailor would look at what last-minute nips and tucks needed to be taken.

Kira turned a slow circle so Kit could see the wedding dress all the way around. "It is pretty, isn't it?" she said, clearly in awe of it herself.

The gown was white satin with a full, floor-length skirt and a fitted, beaded bodice with an off-the-shoulder sweetheart neckline and twenty tiny buttons down the back.

"It's perfect," Kit said.

"Do you think it's okay that the veil only comes down to the my elbows? I didn't want to be dealing with much more than that. Plus I thought a longer veil would detract from the dress."

"I think the veil is fine at that length," Kit assured.

"What about the tiara? Is that too much? I thought maybe the veil should just be attached to a band but it didn't poof up right."

The veil was connected to a small, unobtrusive rhinestone tiara.

"No, it's not too much," Kit answered after a more studied look at it. "It's just right. The whole thing is just right."

"You're sure? Because I'm trusting you to tell me the truth."

"What would you do if I said something was wrong? Start looking for a new dress and veil four days before the wedding?" Kit joked. Then she said, "Yes, I'm positive—the dress, the veil, the tiara are perfect. The dress just needs to be taken in slightly at the waist."

Staring at herself in the mirror, Kira pulled the waist tighter. "It can probably go in about an inch."

"But that's it. I wouldn't change another thing," Kit said emphatically.

Apparently it was emphatic enough to finally convince her friend because Kira transferred her attention to Kit then.

"How about your dress?" Kira asked. "Do you still like it?"

Kira had come back to Denver so they could shop together for Kit's dress. Then Kira had taken it back to Northbridge with her and Kit hadn't seen it since.

"If anything I like it even more than I did when we bought it," she said, taking a turn looking in the mirror. "I'd tried on so many by the time we found it that I was in a fog and I'd forgotten just how pretty it is."

Kit wasn't lying about that, either. She honestly did love the dress she would be wearing for the wedding. In fact, she loved it so much she thought it was something she genuinely might wear on another occasion.

The light-as-air fabric was a coffee-with-cream color, embroidered with a delicate pattern of earth tone wildflowers. It was a spaghetti-strapped chemise that skimmed her figure enticingly all the way to the floor. The neckline was straight across but just low enough for a hint of cleavage to show, and the built-in bra and slight drape of fabric at the bustline gave the illusion that Kit was slightly bigger than she actually was.

"It looks so good on you," Kira said. "The hem needs

to go up a little, but other than that it doesn't have to have a thing done to it.

"It's comfortable, too. It's like I'm just wearing a slip," Kit said, wiggling a little to feel the dress shimmer around her.

Kira glanced at the door the tailor had disappeared through after showing them to the dressing rooms, but that didn't make the short, pudgy man reappear.

And since it didn't, Kira said, "I can't believe it—are we actually going to have some downtime?"

"Maybe we should lock the door and just hide out here."

"Wouldn't that be nice? Peace and quiet? No demands? No schedules? No nothing?" Kira said.

But of course neither of them moved to the door to lock it.

Kira did seem to focus solely on Kit for the first time since Kit's arrival in Northbridge, though. "So, since we have a few minutes, are you okay in the apartment and with everything that's been going on?"

"Everything that's been going on?" Kit repeated, thinking instantly of Ad and how her friend must have noticed the odd energy that seemed to swirl around them whenever they were together.

But that wasn't what Kira was referring to.

"Are you okay with having to be in on all these annoying wedding details?" Kira clarified. "And my not having two minutes for us to just sit and talk and catch up? Having to stay in the apartment instead of with me? Everything?"

"Ah," Kit said, readjusting her thinking and squashing that initial hope that her friend was giving her an opening. But that wasn't the case. And even though it was tempting to talk to Kira about the confusion that Kit was suffering over Ad, she refrained. The more she'd realized how swamped Kira was, the more it had seemed selfish to burden her with some silly fretting. So, sometime during the day, Kit had decided she wouldn't do that. And she didn't go back on that decision now.

Instead, still opting to spare her friend, she said, "Ad's apartment is fine. I didn't come here expecting you to be able to just sit around and gab. I knew you'd be busy. I'm here to help, remember? Not to be entertained."

"I know. I just feel guilty that I'm in this whirl and everything is about me."

Kit laughed. "You're the *bride*. Everything is *supposed* to be about you."

Which was true and saying it only reinforced in Kit's mind that she needed to keep to herself the little attraction or infatuation or whatever it was that rumbled around in her whenever she was with Ad.

But even so, his name came up.

"You seem to keep getting thrown together with Ad," Kira said then. "Is that okay?"

"I'm the maid of honor and he's the best man—getting thrown together is sort of unavoidable, isn't it?" Kit reasoned.

But still her friend didn't drop it. "Staying in his apartment with him just next door, using his kitchen for the cake—you're having to see more of him than just being the maid of honor and best man. Is that all right? I mean, you didn't look like you were having too bad a time on Saturday night when Cutty and I finally got to the restaurant—neither of you even noticed that we'd shown up—but are you hating seeing so much of him? Should I make something up to get us out of dinner with him tonight so you don't have to be with him again?"

"No, don't do that," Kit said, putting some effort into not sounding as alarmed as she felt by just the possibility of canceling dinner with Ad. "He's trying to do something nice for you and Cutty—to give you a relaxing night away from everything. And I don't mind seeing him again. He's a nice guy."

Kira smiled a bit slyly. "I was kind of hoping you two might like each other. You know—really like each other," she finished with a question in her tone.

"I think we like each other well enough."

"Well enough to fall madly in love and get married so you can come and live in Northbridge, too?" Kira joked.

"No, not *that* well enough," Kit countered the same way.

"But you *do* like him?"

"He's a nice guy," Kit repeated.

"Because Cutty was wondering if this dinner tonight was a cover."

"A cover?"

"You know—a group thing to cover up the fact that Ad really just wanted to have dinner with you."

"Oh, I don't think so," Kit said.

And she didn't. She believed Ad's motives for arranging the dinner tonight were exactly what he'd said they were, to give Kira and Cutty a break.

But it did give Kit a twinge of pleasure to entertain that other possibility. "He's seen plenty of me," she added in spite of it. "He's doing this for you guys."

Kira just smiled.

The door to the fitting room opened and the tailor came in just then, putting an end to the conversation before it could go any farther.

But even as Kit watched Kira's gown being pulled and pinned, and even as the hem was turned up on her own dress, she still couldn't suppress a tiny thrill at even the suggestion that Ad had had her in mind when he'd devised the evening to come.

No matter how hard she tried.

Ad and Cutty left the alteration shop after they had finished having their tuxedos fitted and went to the restaurant to wait for Kit and Kira.

The dinner rush had begun by then but they found two free spots to stand at the bar and ordered beers.

"We missed you at that last game," Ad was saying to Cutty as his bartender slid frigid bottles in their direction. "Their pitcher had an arm that wouldn't quit. Struck half of us out and didn't even break a sweat."

Ad and Cutty—and several of the other men in town—played seasonal sports on a local team. Summer was softball season and it was in full swing. But Cutty hadn't been able to participate since breaking his ankle and even though the cast had been removed the week before, he was still in physical therapy.

They each took a swig of beer and replaced their bottles on the bar.

"So tomorrow night you're just coming to watch? You really can't play?" Ad asked.

"I really can't," Cutty answered. "Kira and the physical therapist ganged up on me. The ankle can be pretty wobbly still and they pointed out that I shouldn't risk doing damage with everything that's coming up."

"They didn't want you limping down the aisle," Ad said.

"Or messing up the honeymoon," Cutty added with a cat-that-ate-the-canary grin. "I agreed with that part of it."

"I'll bet you did."

They drank more beer and tossed back a few of the complimentary peanuts from the bowl in front of them.

"We really appreciate you having Kit stay in the apartment," Cutty said then. "Our guest room is construction central—it's full of tools and paint cans and light fixtures. It's a mess. And I don't know where we would have put all the stuff if we had to clear it out for her—the garage is packed, too. That's where the wallboard and the new bathtub and the sinks and the rest of the plumbing supplies are."

"It's no big deal," Ad assured. "The place was empty anyway. Why shouldn't she use it?"

"Yeah, but you've been picking up the slack for us

as hosts, too. I didn't mean for you to have to entertain her but—"

"I'm hardly entertaining her. She's with Kira most of the time. I just did a little kitchen duty last night is all."

"And you picked her up at the bus station and kept her company for us when we were getting Mel stitched up."

"No big deal."

"Yeah, well I owe you."

"Believe me, you really don't," Ad said slightly under his breath, thinking that none of the time he'd spent with Kit had been a hardship on him. In fact, it had been the opposite.

Maybe that had somehow echoed in his tone because it drew a curious look from his friend.

But Cutty didn't comment on it, and Ad didn't expound. Instead they both raised their bottles to their mouths again.

When they'd set them down once more Cutty said, "This was a good idea tonight. I've been so damn busy it seems like ten years since we've just had a beer and a burger."

"Buying a new house, moving, remodeling, getting married—that'll keep you occupied all right."

"'Course I did wonder if it was really my company and Kira's you were after tonight. Or if maybe you'd just worked up a plan to get a little Kit-time in for yourself—if maybe you've *liked* picking up the slack for us."

Ad gave his friend a sideways glance. "That's what you were wondering, huh?"

"Is it true?"

"I invite you for a beer, a little dinner, and you think I have ulterior motives," Ad joked, pretending he was injured by the suggestion.

"Uh-huh. I notice you aren't denying it, though. Could it be you're interested in Kit?" Cutty asked.

"She's an interesting enough person. We have some things in common—restaurant work for instance."

"Uh-huh," Cutty repeated. "So you're definitely interested."

Ad took another drink of beer. Then he said, "Nah."

"Okay. Let me put it a different way. If Kit had been born and raised in Northbridge, would you definitely be interested?"

"Definitely?" Ad hedged.

"Would you be interested?" Cutty said insistently.

"Maybe," was the most Ad would concede. But it wasn't because he was playing games with his friend. He really didn't want to give in to being attracted to Kit, and it seemed as if admitting anything to Cutty would be the first step in letting down his guard.

"But since she *isn't* a permanent fixture around here, you aren't interested?" Cutty finished for him.

"Right."

Cutty ate some more nuts. "Seems like the number of Northbridge women on your dance card is pretty low."

"I've been out with a few," Ad claimed defensively.

"One or two dates. You've already seen Kit twice and

here we are tonight—you've bent over backward to arrange number three."

"I didn't bend over backward. I called you and said why don't we have dinner after the fitting. How is that bending over backward?"

Now he *really* sounded defensive.

Ad slammed back some peanuts and washed them down with beer.

"I'm just thinking that maybe you need to reconsider this rule of yours that prohibits getting into anything with any out-of-town women."

Actually, in the last three days Ad had done a surprising amount of just that. But always with the same conclusion.

"It's a good rule. I'm sticking to it," he told his friend.

"Kira's from out of town. She's moved here and loves it," Cutty said.

"And I hope that's the way it always is. For your sake."

"But you won't run the risk."

"Once burned, twice shy," Ad said.

"Too bad," Cutty mused with a shake of his head. "Kit seems like someone pretty special."

"She's also someone with a whole business in Denver. And why are we even talking about this, anyway?"

"Whoa-ho! The man's back is up!" Cutty goaded, pretending to be intimidated by the impatient note that had slipped into Ad's tone.

But the impatience wasn't really aimed at his friend. It was born of his own frustration because Ad agreed with Cutty—Kit did seem like someone pretty special.

She seemed a lot better than pretty special. And he *had* had her and getting to see her tonight in mind when he'd devised this dinner.

It just didn't change anything. Nothing was going to change anything. And he knew it. He kept reminding himself of it.

And then he did things like this anyway.

Things he still felt like he had to defend.

"Okay, I'm not having any trouble being around your maid of honor," he acknowledged reluctantly. "But it's perfectly innocent—"

"Which is part of why Kira and I agreed to tonight—to keep it innocent."

Ad rolled his eyes as if that didn't have anything to do with it when, in fact, it was the second of his two reasons for this dinner. Cutty knew him too well.

But still he wouldn't go too much farther. "I like Kit fine, no more, no less than a lot of people. Now can we drop this and talk about something else?"

Cutty shrugged. "Sure," he agreed, with a knowing smile that just made Ad shake his head again.

And so what if, in the process he managed to steal a glimpse at the restaurant's front door and feel a wave of hope that Kit would be coming through it soon?

It didn't mean anything.

Or so he told himself.

Kira's remark about Ad arranging for Kira, Cutty, Kit and himself to have dinner so he could be with Kit stayed with Kit all through the evening.

Still, the food was wonderful, the conversation was lively and upbeat, and the two bottles of wine they went through should have kept her from dwelling on such a minor thing.

Yet Kit couldn't get the comment out of her head. She just kept considering the possibility that it was true.

Had Ad arranged this dinner to spend time with her?

And if he had, did that mean he might feel a little tug in her direction the way she felt in his?

It was silly to be so titillated by the thought. Especially when she was fighting that tug with all her might. But she just couldn't help it.

Anymore than she could help looking for signs that Cutty hadn't been imagining things and that Ad had had her in mind when he'd suggested this dinner.

She didn't see any signs of it, though. There wasn't a single instance in which Ad showed her any more attention than he showed Kira or Cutty. There wasn't a single glance that seemed particularly pointed or meaningful. There was nothing but an openly-in-love couple and their two friends having a meal and wine together and talking the evening away.

Which was just as it should have been. Just as Kit wanted it to be…

"What do you see in this guy?" Ad asked Kira as the evening was winding down and the restaurant staff was closing up around them.

"Hey!" Cutty protested before Kira could respond. He had just made a bad joke that had left them all laughing and groaning at the same time.

"You're sure you want to marry him?" Ad persisted.

"I might have to give it a second thought," Kira said, playing along.

"Hey to you, too," Cutty complained.

"Well, you know," Kira continued to joke, "painful puns and a weak ankle and you do snore sometimes—maybe I *should* reconsider."

Cutty shot a mock frown in Kit's direction. "Did you give her your wedding willies?" he demanded.

"Don't look at me," Kit protested. "If she has wedding willies, she got them on her own."

"Wedding willies?" Ad repeated. "What are wedding willies?"

"You know," Cutty explained, "fear of weddings."

"You specialize in wedding cakes but you're afraid of weddings?" Ad said to Kit.

"Only her own," Cutty supplied, sounding slightly tipsy.

"Cutty!" Kira reprimanded. Then, to Kit and Ad, she said, "I think I'd better take him home before he puts his foot in his mouth."

Cutty's expression turned sheepish. "Was I not supposed to say that?" he asked, sounding confused. "It's only Ad. I can say anything to Ad."

"No, you can't." Kira glanced at Kit and made a what-can-you-expect-he's-a-man face. "I'm sorry."

Kit laughed. "It's okay. He's right, I never get nervous at anyone else's wedding."

"I'm still taking him home," Kira insisted, pushing her chair away from the table.

She stood and pulled Cutty with her.

There didn't seem to be any stopping them so Ad and Kit got up, too.

There were chairs on the rest of the tables by then and the four of them wove their way through the jungle of uprooted wooden legs to the front door.

"What's on tomorrow's to-do list?" Kit asked her friend while Ad unlocked the door to let them out.

"The final okay on flower arrangements, and meeting the caterer and the woman who's in charge of the reception. We're meeting her at the church even though the reception will be in the town square, under a tent. I have to figure out where the buffet tables need to be and look over the tablecloths and the place settings. I have to make up my mind about whether the tables and chairs should be at one end of the tent and the dance floor at the other, or if the tables and chairs should be around the perimeters with the dance floor in the center, and—" Kira cut herself off. "There's just a million details I have to make decisions about. I never knew weddings were so much work."

Kit hated to add to her friend's already overwhelming load, but she had to. "We also need to do some shopping for the shower tomorrow night," she reminded.

"That, too," Kira said, clearly having forgotten. "We'd better get an early start—can I pick you up at nine?"

"Sure," Kit answered.

Cutty put his arm around Kira then and together they thanked Ad for dinner and said good-night.

When they'd left, Ad closed the door behind them

and leaned against it as if blocking Kit from following them out even though she needed to leave through the back door rather than the front anyway.

He was dressed in plain jeans and another polo shirt with the restaurant's name on it—this one red—but he still looked good enough to make Kit want to stare.

Which was actually what he was doing to her.

But she didn't think the simple white linen slacks and pink short-sleeved, crew-neck T-shirt she had on were the cause since there was something probing in his gaze.

"Wedding willies?" he said a moment later, out of the blue.

Kit had been afraid that this last part of the evening's conversation had left him too curious to drop it. But Cutty's wedding willies reference was about the last thing she wanted to get into, so rather than addressing it, she said, "Kira was right—we're getting an early start tomorrow. I should probably call it a night, too, and get some sleep." In spite of a nagging reluctance to end the evening yet herself.

"Ah, the subject of wedding willies is *verboten*—I get it," Ad said. Still, he didn't budge from his stance at the door. Or stop watching her.

After another moment he said, "So if I guarantee that I won't ask about it again tonight will you stay and help me finish that last little bit of wine that's left in the bottle?"

It had been great wine. Very expensive wine. It was a shame to let it go to waste…

Okay, Kit knew she was just rationalizing to provide herself with an excuse to stay.

But it was for only a while. Only long enough for one last glass of wine. And it wasn't *that* late, after all. Not quite midnight. And she wasn't tired…

"No wedding willies talk?" she asked.

"Not a word," he promised.

"Okay, then."

Using a combination of broad shoulders and hip action, Ad pushed himself off the door.

Kit then spun around on her heels and returned to the table that they'd been using all evening, as if she hadn't even noticed how lithe and sexy that little motion had been.

There was only enough wine left for half a glass each, and after they'd both reclaimed their chairs at the table Ad poured equal amounts into Kit's glass and his.

"I keep thinking about what you told me last night," she said, wanting to get the conversation off in another direction.

"What did I tell you last night?" he asked.

"About your dad dying when you were so young and how you had to help support your family. I was wondering if you felt robbed of a childhood."

"Not at all," Ad said without hesitation. "I mean, losing my dad was bad, but I had a pretty normal childhood. Northbridge was—and is—a great place to be a kid."

"How so?" Kit asked between sips of her wine.

"It's safer than most places," he said as if it was an obvious answer. "Everyone watches out for everyone else and for everyone else's kids, so parents don't have to keep too tight a rein on their children. They know that wherever their kid is, *somebody* will be nearby to help if they need it or keep them in line if that's what's called for. That translates into more freedom than I think most kids can have. And what kid doesn't want to go off on their own when they can and play and have adventures?"

"Were there a lot of adventures in Northbridge?" Kit asked skeptically since it seemed so unlikely.

"For a kid? Sure. For a kid, everything that isn't being regulated by a parent is an adventure. Riding bikes pretty much anywhere we wanted to go. Long summer days swimming out at the pond. Fishing or tubing in the river. One year we spent until after the fourth of July building a treehouse and then camped out in it every night until school started. On Halloween we'd hit the mother lode for candy. In the winter there was skating on the pond and sledding down Sloan Hill."

It did sound like fun.

"Did you have a lot of friends or did you mainly hang out with your sister and brothers?" Kit inquired while he took a drink of his wine.

"Both. I had a lot of friends, but there was no shortage of playmates at home, either. I don't recall ever being bored or lonely, that's for sure."

"So in spite of losing your dad, you honestly did have a good childhood?"

"I did. In fact my childhood was the kind I want my own kids to have."

Kit had the sense that that was very important to

him. "You really love Northbridge, don't you?" she surmised from the affection in his tone.

"I do. It's the perfect place to live, to have and raise a family."

"But what about when you were a teenager? Didn't you want to break out? Get away from the confines of a small town?"

Ad shrugged, and Kit's gaze rode along like a caress. "Sure, there was some of that. But usually somebody would get hold of a car on a Friday or Saturday night and we'd head for Billings. We'd try—and fail—to get beer, meet some girls, show off at every opportunity. But that would sort of satisfy the yen for city life and then it was nice to head for home when we'd had our fill."

"And you even went to college here?"

"Yep."

"So you've never lived anywhere but Northbridge?" Kit marveled.

"I didn't say that."

But he also didn't say where else he *had* lived. Or when. And Kit had the distinct impression that that was something he didn't want to talk about anymore than she'd wanted to explain her wedding willies.

So she didn't push it.

Instead she said, "What about your family? Are they all still around here?"

"They are. My mom never left the house where we grew up. She could retire but she likes to work now— she manages the town dry cleaners. And my sister and brothers are here, too. In fact, my brother, Ben, just bought a place—it was a home and school for delinquent kids that he's going to reopen."

"Are any of your siblings married?"

Ad finished his wine, shaking his had as he swallowed. "Nope, afraid not."

The *yep* and *nope* made Kit wonder if that final half-glass of wine might have put him over the sober line. She knew it had left her slightly more light-headed than she'd been before. Slightly more light-headed and intensely aware of every little detail about him.

Too intensely aware of every little detail about him, she realized suddenly.

In an attempt to fight it, she pushed herself away from the table and stood.

"Well, the wine is gone and you know what that means?" she said by way of explaining the abrupt change of position.

"You're deserting me all of a sudden?" Ad said, sounding surprised and bereaved.

"I'm afraid so. We polished off the wine and you heard Kira—I have to be out and about early tomorrow."

"Evil wedding," he said in mock condemnation.

But he stood, too.

Together they took the four glasses and the empty bottle into the kitchen that had been cleaned before the staff left.

"Give me a minute and I'll walk you upstairs," Ad said, disposing of the bottle and putting the glasses in the big, industrial dishwasher.

It was a sight Kit paid closer attention to than she

should have. The wide span of his shoulders formed the top of a V that evolved into hips and a derriere that sat snuggly cupped by the pockets of his jeans. And she enjoyed the view. A lot.

"All set," he announced when he was done, turning to face her.

At first Kit wasn't sure if he'd caught her with her eyes on his rear end or if she'd managed to raise them in time. But when she saw the tiny smile that tweaked the corners of his mouth she knew she hadn't fooled him.

Embarrassment pushed her out the alley door just as he headed for it.

The night air was warm and humid but Kit breathed deeply, hoping it would help put her in a more rational state of mind.

It didn't, though, because when Ad joined her outside a moment later he brought with him the lingering scent of his cologne and it was this that she was focused on more than the fresh air by the time he'd locked the door behind them.

"So Kira's wedding shower is tomorrow night," Ad said as they climbed the steps, making small talk.

"Right," Kit confirmed, forcing herself to pay attention.

"We have a softball game," Ad informed her. "Cutty can't play yet but he's coming to watch so he'll be out of your way."

"Good, because it's girls only."

They reached the landing then, and Kit unlocked the door to the studio apartment and turned to face him to say goodbye.

He was standing closer than she'd realized. There they were, accidentally face-to-face, separated by mere inches.

Of course, either of them could have moved to put more distance between them, but neither of them did.

Neither of them said anything, either, and Kit wasn't quite sure why that was.

Just say good-night, she told herself. *Just say good-night and go inside.*

But still she didn't. She merely stood there, looking up into Ad's finely honed features…almost as if she were expecting something.

Just say good-night! she repeated to herself.

"Between leaving early in the morning and not coming back until after the shower I probably won't see you at all tomorrow…" she said instead, not understanding why.

Ad only acknowledged it with an arch of his brows because he was too intent on studying her face, on searching her eyes.

Still, Kit felt the urge to say more so she said, "I hope you have a good game."

"Thanks. I hope you have a good shower."

"Me, too…" she said, her voice trailing off because she was beginning to wonder if he was somehow even closer than he'd been a moment earlier. If he was coming closer even now. If he was slowly bending down. If he might be about to kiss her.

She honestly wasn't sure.

But for some reason her chin raised a fraction of an inch on its own just the same.

I shouldn't be doing this, she thought.

But her chin went up another fraction of an inch.

It must have been the wine. I shouldn't have had that last half-glass.

But up went her chin another tiny bit.

Only Ad didn't come any closer.

In fact, his almost imperceptible descent stalled with his face, his mouth scant inches from hers.

Then he straightened up completely.

"You wanted to go in," he said abruptly, as if he'd just remembered that.

Or maybe what he'd just remembered was himself.

Either way, with that he moved even farther from her, heading for his own door. "G'night."

Kit raised her chin higher still in acknowledgment of that but her mouth was too dry for her to speak. The most she managed was a small wave, hoping it looked as if the thought of him kissing her hadn't even crossed her mind.

Then she went into her apartment, closed the door behind her and wilted a little.

Maybe he'd just been taking a closer look at something on her face, she told herself. Maybe he'd thought there was a bug on her nose. Maybe he hadn't been on the verge of kissing her at all…

But she didn't really believe that.

She didn't believe that her sense that he'd been about to kiss her had been wrong.

And she couldn't help feeling let down that he hadn't actually done it.

Chapter Four

"The Northbridge Bruisers? I think that team should be the Northbridge Babes. Or the Northbridge Hunks. It's a testament to how highly I think of you, Kira, that I'm here at your shower rather than at that field, watching that softball game."

"Amen to that!"

"Oh, so true!"

"We're missing Buns On Parade just for you!"

It was late the next evening; Kira's wedding shower had been going on for hours and, of the thirty guests, the older contingent had already gone home and the twenty or so who were left were the younger women who had been invited. And thanks to the three bowls of heavily spiked punch, no one—including Kit—was feeling any pain, which had prompted a conversation about the local, year-round, informal sports team that both Ad and Cutty belonged to.

"Come on," Kit said, "they can't all be that great-looking."

Laughter was her answer, accompanied by a "That's what you think—" and a "You have to see it to believe it."

"I told you after the first game I went to," Kira contributed, "that most of the team is made up of fabulous-looking, single guys. It's like there's something in the water around here."

The presents had all been opened, the food had been served from a buffet table still laden with the leftovers, and three of the attendees had been adorned in toilet-paper wedding dresses as one of the games that had been played. Kit, as well as the other two, had retained most of their getups as everyone lounged around on the sofa, chairs and the pillows tossed on the floor.

"I think you all just sit in the hot sun on the bleachers getting sloshed, and that's what makes the whole team look so good," Kit accused.

"Not true," one of the women defended. "When you have that much beefcake to look at, who needs booze?"

More laughter rippled through the group.

"What's your favorite season?" someone asked the room in general in a tone that invited confidences.

"Not softball," someone else answered. "The uniforms aren't tight enough and they cover too much."

That garnered a combination of roaring laughter and agreement.

"Give me football season and those butt-hugging

tight-things they wear for pants," another of the guests chimed in.

"That's good," a short, freckle-faced woman said from the corner, "but basketball has to be the best— shorts and tank tops. All those muscley thighs and biceps. I live for basketball season."

"You're all terrible," Kit told them, laughing as she did. "I'll bet these guys think you come to watch the games and you're really just there to ogle them."

"Absolutely."

"Don't kid yourself, they love it."

More laughter.

"Not that we're gawking at Cutty now that he's spoken for," the town manicurist assured Kira. "But at least we still have the Walker brothers."

A moan of appreciation went up at that.

"Ad Walker is the one I sit up front for," a secretary from the local college contributed.

Kit had been in on this conversation the whole way but that comment increased her interest a hundredfold.

The secretary continued. "I don't know what it takes to get him to notice me, though. I've eaten a river of fish and a mountain of chips at his restaurant hoping he'd give me a second glance and all I have to show for it is the five pounds I've gained."

More laughter. From everyone but Kit.

The secretary, Amanda Barnes, was tall, long-legged, and if she'd put on weight it must have been in her chest because nothing else on the blond, blue-eyed beauty showed any excess. It was difficult to believe Ad hadn't noticed her, and Kit wondered if he just didn't realize the secretary had set her cap for him.

But knowing that cap was set for him didn't sit particularly well with Kit. Even though she knew it shouldn't matter to her.

"Ad's brothers are no slouches, either," someone else added. "Those boys must come from good genes because one is better-looking than the other."

"They've got good *jeans,* all right, and boy-oh-boy, can they fill them out."

Laughter rippled again, and someone did a wolf whistle.

"Ad is hot, but me, I'd go for Ben Walker," the manicurist said with a mock swoon. "Give me a bad boy every time."

A few Mmms of agreement went up at that.

"Ad is Cutty's best friend, isn't he, Kira?" the secretary said.

"He has been since Cutty came to Northbridge," Kira confirmed.

"So couldn't you arrange something for me? A blind date or a dinner with him or something?"

"Not Kira, she wouldn't do that," Kit heard herself say before she even knew she was going to open her mouth. But now that she had, she had to make it good. "Kira will never do fix-ups. Will you, Kira?"

"I won't?" Kira said.

"Why not?" the manicurist demanded.

Kira didn't have an answer for something Kit had made up on the spot so Kit answered for her. "She set me up once with a horrible guy and swore off all match-making from then on."

"That's right," Kira said, a little late on the uptake, casting Kit a look that said Kit was going to have some explaining to do.

But not now. Now she just needed to get the subject changed.

"What are we doing talking about a sports team at a wedding shower, anyway?" Kit joked. "We're supposed to be talking about Kira and the wedding. And drinking punch. Who's ready for more punch?" she asked enthusiastically, getting up from her spot on the floor.

She was glad that several women admitted they wouldn't turn down another glass.

"Just give me five minutes to refill the bowl," she said. Then, to urge the conversation in a different direction, she added, "While I'm gone, Kira can tell you where she and Cutty are going on their honeymoon."

"Tahiti," Kira announced, taking her cue as Kit sought some refuge in her friend's kitchen. She couldn't believe she'd just said and done what she'd said and done.

Why had she said and done it? she asked herself as she set the bowl on the counter and opened the refrigerator.

Taking out a pitcher of the margarita-like punch, she wondered if that was the culprit. Maybe the liquor in the punch had just made her say and do things without thinking. Things she had no business saying or doing at all.

It certainly wasn't her place to keep someone from dating Ad. Or to keep Kira from arranging it. Who Ad dated didn't have anything to do with Kit. There was no law against the college secretary exploring the possibility of a relationship with him. Obviously she liked Ad. And he might like her if he got to know her. They might hit it off, fall madly in love, get married and have a dozen kids and live happily ever after. None of it was Kit's business. None of it should make any difference to her.

So why had she interfered? Why had she been so intent on preventing it from happening?

It had almost been a panic reaction. Instinct. As if she'd been protecting her territory.

But that was ridiculous. Ad wasn't her territory.

Maybe that's where the punch had come into play, she thought as she poured it into the bowl. Maybe it had caused an irrational sense that Ad was her territory and the equally irrational response of protecting that territory.

The punch. Yes, it must have been the punch.

Or the niggling attraction to him that had been tormenting her since she'd met him.

Of those two possibilities she preferred to blame the liquor. Otherwise it would mean that she'd been jealous of the idea of another woman having a chance with Ad and that was so much more complicated. Kit just didn't want to even entertain the idea.

No, it was the punch. So, no more punch for her.

She should go back out there and undo what she'd done, she told herself. She should go back out there and encourage Kira to break that made-up rule and get Ad and the secretary together. It was the right thing to do.

Yet every time Kit pictured Ad with Amanda Barnes,

the image cut her like a knife. And she knew that, right or wrong, she couldn't be the one to help Amanda Barnes get her hands on Ad.

If they're meant to be together, they'll find each other.

But still she muttered to herself, "You're a horrible person, Kit MacIntyre."

A horrible person who should probably have felt guiltier about it.

But all she really felt was relief that, at least for the time being, Ad and Amanda Barnes were not on the path to each other.

In fact, she felt so much relief that a wave of silliness overtook her.

Among Kira's presents there had been a few gag gifts. Kit had no idea how one of them had gotten into the kitchen, but spotting the bra with the hard cone cups with the tassels attached to the tips of each one, she picked it up and put it on her head, tying the ends under her chin to keep it in place.

Then, with the full punch bowl cradled in both hands, she charged out of the kitchen, calling, "More punch," before she actually looked out into the living room.

And what she discovered was that while she'd been gone, several uninvited guests had arrived—Cutty, Ad and a large contingent of men Kit could only guess were members of the Northbridge Bruisers team.

"Oh!"

All eyes had turned to her. And there she was, with two bra-cup cones sticking out from the sides of her head, the tassels dangling down over her ears, face-to-face with a number of men whom she'd never met, as well as Cutty and—to her greatest horror—Ad.

If she'd been able to, the first thing she would have done was snatch that bra off her head. But as it was, she just stood there, frozen to the spot as male and female laughter erupted and a man's voice called out a lascivious, "Nice hat."

There was nothing Kit could do but bluff her way out of it, so she said, "Thanks," as if she didn't mind at all that a whole bunch of men were seeing her with a bra on her head.

Then she headed for the buffet table. All the way across the room.

"What kind of party are you having here?" another of the men said over the laughter as she wove her way through the throng of big, good-looking galoots.

"You didn't know we went wild when you weren't around, did you?" the manicurist answered.

"I told the guys the party was probably about over and we could see if there was any food left. I didn't expect a floor show, too," Cutty said.

Kit finally reached the buffet table and set the bowl down. The moment she could, she slipped the bra from her head, but with all eyes still on her, she wasn't sure what to do with it. She considered stashing it behind the pile of presents in the corner, but somehow it seemed as if doing that would be admitting embarrassment, and admitting embarrassment might only make this all more embarrassing.

So she opted for toughing it out to the end—she

hooked a strap around one index finger, swung the bra until she had some momentum and let it fly into the group.

Apparently no one had expected her to do that. But the fact that she had was a crowd-pleaser. More laughter roared, there were some hoots and hollers, and another wolf whistle.

Kit didn't know what had been going on before her reappearance in the living room, but if there had been any question about the men staying or joining the festivities that seemed to provide the answer. Because suddenly several women moved over to make room for men to sit beside them, and some women stood and began to mingle among those left standing.

"I guess you can stay," Kira announced to Cutty as she went to him to kiss him hello.

Feeling as if she'd weathered the storm, Kit relaxed and began to scan the now-milling people in search of Ad. Just to say hello, she told herself.

Which was what it looked like he was coming toward her to do himself when his path was blocked by Amanda Barnes.

Kit didn't know why, but she suddenly felt as awkward as a junior high-school girl returning a wave that had been intended for the person behind her.

"I'd better get more glasses and plates," she said to no one in particular and beat a hasty retreat to the kitchen again.

But once she was there she couldn't help peering back into the living room from the distance.

Kira and her Northbridge friends had been right

about the team—not a single man lacked head-turning qualities. But it was only Ad who Kit was curious about.

Ad, who was standing in the middle of the living room with Amanda Barnes.

All the men looked as if they'd just showered after their game and Ad was no different. He had on a pair of snug-fitting jeans and a plain white mock-turtleneck T-shirt that curved over each and every muscle.

That wasn't lost on the secretary, whose gaze kept lingering on his pectorals. When she wasn't laying a hand to one of his forearms, which were bared by sleeves pushed above his elbows.

The sight of Amanda Barnes touching Ad riled something in Kit that she hadn't even known she possessed. It left her inclined to rush out there, throw herself between them and get the secretary to back off.

But of course she couldn't do that.

She could only stand there and watch as Amanda Barnes smiled and chatted and put her hands on Ad.

It had all just worked out so well for the secretary. Kit had to wonder if fate had intervened to bring Ad and Amanda together right under her nose and in spite of her best efforts to prevent it. Perhaps this was an indication that they really were meant to find each other and a warning to her to butt out.

Okay, fine, let them have each other, she thought.

They did make an attractive couple. They were both tall, long-limbed, bright-eyed and athletic. They were probably perfect for each other. They were about the same age. They lived in the same town—a town small enough for them to no doubt know the same people. For them to frequent the same places. They might even have the same interests. The same goals. They might be totally suited for each other. And there was no mistaking the fact that Amanda had her cap set for Ad.

Damn her, anyway. Her and that sleek, shiny, manageable hair she kept flipping around as if she were filming a shampoo commercial.

It finally occurred to Kit that she was only torturing herself by standing there to witness what was happening, and she spun away from the doorway.

As she did she caught sight of herself reflected in the side of the toaster and realized that not only had she appeared a few moments earlier with a bra on her head, but that she was also still wearing the toilet-paper wedding dress.

"Smooth. Really smooth," she said sarcastically, going to work tearing off the tissue.

Underneath it she had on a pair of khaki slacks and a wine-colored camp shirt that didn't compare to the tight capri pants and the sexy tube-top Amanda Barnes was nearly spilling out of. But it was still better than a toilet-paper wedding dress.

When she had finally torn it all off and done some damage control to her hair, the sides of which were pulled up to the top of her head while the rest fell around her shoulders, she put the paper in the trash.

As she did, she reminded herself that she had sworn off men and hadn't come to Northbridge to find one. That it was good—no, it was great—if Ad discovered the college secretary who had been trying to get his attention, and they *did* live happily ever after.

"Save me!"

Kit jumped in startled fright and jerked around to find Ad in the kitchen doorway. Without Amanda Barnes.

"Save you?" Kit repeated.

He subtly nodded over his shoulder. "Amanda Barnes," he said under his breath. "I barely escaped with my life. I think she's stalking me."

Kit had to laugh. Not only because of the way he said that and the notion of the big man being intimidated by the secretary who had eyes for him, but also because a second round of relief washed through her tonight.

"She's stalking you?" Kit said as if she hadn't had any idea anything was going on.

"She moved to town about six months ago and has been driving me crazy ever since. She comes to the restaurant and asks to have me sent to her table like I'm one of the appetizers on the menu. She comes to our games and then stands outside the locker room to nab me when I leave so she can rehash all my plays. Sometimes I think she lays in wait for me around town because she has an inordinate knack for showing up wherever I am, and now here she is again. I'm telling you, I can't get away from her."

"Maybe you should stop trying," Kit suggested, offering fate a hand.

Ad crossed the kitchen to stand nearer to her and then leaned forward to confide in her. "I don't like her."

Okay, so that pleased Kit far more than it should have.

"And you shouldn't like her, either," Ad continued. "She's an enemy of sugar. She never eats dessert. I think she's from another planet."

Kit was trying not to smile too big. "So what do you want me to do? Hide you in the pantry?"

That made him grin a one-sided, mischievous grin. "Hmm. I don't know. Will you hide in there with me?"

He couldn't be aware of how tempting an idea that actually was to her.

But all she said was, "I don't think so," just as Amanda Barnes appeared in the doorway.

"I thought you were coming in here for a quick drink of water, not to talk to Kit. Do you need help?" the other woman asked.

Ad turned from Kit to Amanda and said, "No, thanks, I think I can get my own drink of water. But don't let me keep you, because after that I'm going to make good on my promise to Cutty to introduce Kit to all the guys. You know—it's kind of a best man-maid of honor thing."

Before Amanda could say anything to that, Kit added, "Cutty and Kira keep depending on Ad to look after me since they're both so busy."

Amanda was obviously unhappy to hear that. Her eyes went from Ad to Kit and back to Ad, and her expression was suspicious. But she didn't have much choice, she couldn't refute their claim.

"Come find me when you're finished," she said to Ad then, her tone full of insinuation.

Ad just gave her a halfhearted lift of the chin in answer. But apparently Amanda Barnes didn't notice how halfhearted it was or that there was no commitment on his part because she tossed him a seductive wink, spun around on her heels to give him the view of her backside and walked away with a pronounced sway of her hips.

"Every instinct I have tells me that woman is a man-eater," Ad confided quietly when Amanda was gone.

"Coward," Kit teased. "And what was that part about Cutty making you introduce me around?"

"That part was a lie, pure and simple," he admitted. "But now we'll have to do it because you can bet she'll be watching and will pounce on me again if I'm not really, really busy with you."

"Ah, I see. So you're using me," Kit said, pretending offense when she was actually glad for the excuse to have Ad to herself.

"It's in the wedding handbook, if you would have read it, you'd know," he deadpanned. "Rule number seven— It's the duty of the maid of honor to protect the best man from predatory females who use wedding events as opportunities to pick up groomsmen."

"The wedding handbook?"

"Don't tell me you didn't get your copy? Remind me and I'll loan you mine."

Kit laughed again. "You are bad."

His grin this time wasn't merely one-sided. "Only a little. Now come on, let's make this look good," he said, sweeping one arm wide so she could go ahead of him back to the living room.

"Okay, but you owe me."

"Anything," he said, as if he wouldn't mind paying up.

Ad didn't leave Kit's side for the remainder of the evening, but she wasn't complaining. Even though she did meet several of his friends—who were not only jaw-droppingly handsome but also nice and funny and charming and very down-to-earth—she still didn't have the desire to be with anyone but Ad because no matter how handsome, nice, funny, charming or down-to-earth the other guys were, none of them strummed that same chord in her that Ad did.

The party lasted another hour before guests began to leave. Kit and Ad stayed until everyone else had gone— including Amanda Barnes, who ordered Ad to call her sometime. Then Cutty, Ad, Kira and Kit all pitched in to put the house back in order.

Once they'd accomplished that, Cutty took his car keys out of his pocket, intent on driving Ad and Kit home, because somehow, during the course of the evening, Ad had ended up without a car.

But rather than accepting the ride, Ad turned to Kit and said, "How about if we walk? I know it's almost a mile, but it's a nice night and I'm game if you are."

It was late and Kit had put in a long day but still the idea of a walk with Ad was appealing. "Okay, but if Amanda Barnes jumps out of the bushes to attack you, I'm not protecting you," she warned.

"It's a deal."

They said good-night to Cutty and Kira and left, stepping out into the balmy silence of the night where they were the only people on the house-lined streets.

In fact, the streets were so deserted that they left the sidewalk to stroll down the middle of the road.

"I haven't been out walking around at this time of night since I was a teenager," Kit said as they settled into a leisurely pace, side by side.

"Uh-oh, that's not the vision I had of you," Ad joked. "What were you doing out walking around at this time of night when you were a teenager?"

"It was part of my misspent youth," Kit said to play along.

"Really?" Ad asked, sounding intrigued by the possibility.

"What vision did you have of me?" she challenged wryly.

"A white-picket-fence, sheltered upbringing. I figured you came from an ordinary family—a mom, a dad, two-point-something kids, a couple cats, a dog, a gerbil and strict rules to live by. But now? I'm wondering."

"We did have a gerbil and a dog, but only one cat and no white picket fence. And there were four kids, not just two-point-something. But you were close—we were definitely an ordinary family and there were a lot of rules. But most of them got broken once or twice."

"Your three siblings—brothers? Sisters? A combination?" Ad asked.

"Sisters."

"Four girls?" he said as if that intrigued him, too.

"Even the dog and the cat were female. We used to joke that my dad lived in a house of women," she said, as if it were something lurid.

"Lucky man."

"I don't think he always thought so. You haven't seen war until you've seen four teenage girls fighting."

"You and your sisters didn't get along?" Ad asked.

"We're great friends now, but as kids, we competed and swiped each other's things, and sabotaged each other, and tattled, and got each other into trouble, and stole each other's boyfriends and—"

"Okay, I change my opinion—your poor father."

Kit laughed. "He spent a lot of time in the garage."

"I'll bet. So are your folks still alive and kicking after all that?"

"They are. They retired to Arizona three years ago. Believe it or not now they're very big into competitive ballroom dancing."

"Competitive ballroom dancing?"

"We can't figure it out," Kit said with an affectionate laugh. "They didn't even have a band at their wedding because my mom said neither one of them knew how to dance at all. Then my dad retired from his sales job and my mom retired from nursing and all of a sudden they decided to take lessons. It just snowballed from there. They travel all over the country. My mom has a whole closet full of gowns with all kinds of petticoats so the skirts will fly out just so, and it's a whole new lease on life for them."

"Maybe after raising four mean daughters they needed to cut loose," Ad suggested with a chuckle.

"We definitely gave them gray hair," Kit confirmed.

"Who was the worst?"

"Never tell anyone I admitted this—my whole family says it and I always deny it—but I'm the oldest and I was the worst."

Ad cast her a disbelieving glance. "You?"

"Me."

"Didn't anyone ever tell you that the oldest is supposed to set a good example?"

"Everyone told me that. Over and over again. It just didn't stick."

"So what did you do?" Ad asked, as if she needed to prove to him just how bad she'd been.

"When I was little I got into the most mischief—I ate bugs—"

"You're first culinary explorations?"

"Maybe. I was also the tree-climber in the family—climbing and falling out. I hit my sisters, broke their toys, and once I talked my youngest sister into sticking her head between the rungs of an heirloom rocking chair and then we couldn't get her out and the chair had to be sawed in half—just your basic mischief-making."

"And what about when you got older?"

"Climbing was still a big thing with me, although then it was climbing out of my bedroom window after everybody was asleep. Before I could drive I'd meet up with my friends and basically just walk around, hang out—that's what this reminds me of."

"What else?" Ad asked, clearly getting a kick out of this.

"My parents had a rule that I couldn't wear makeup until I was sixteen. I thought that was waaa-ay too late, so I put it on and took it off at school. In the seventh grade. Until I got tattled on. I had a boyfriend who drove a motorcycle—"

"Not a motorcycle!" Ad said in mock horror.

"And at various times when my sisters told on me, I had some less than divine retributions."

"Such as?"

"It was one of my sisters who squealed about the makeup and while she slept that night I cut off a chunk of her hair. Once, another of my sisters got me into trouble for skipping school to go to the movies and while *she* slept I colored the tip of her nose with a black marker so it looked like a puppy dog's nose—only I used a permanent marker. The day before we were supposed to take our family picture for our Christmas cards."

"You were very busy."

"I was," she agreed.

"Was there more?"

"There were incidents of locking sisters in the basement so I could have a party while my parents were gone, and clipping every few stitches of the seam down the back of one of my sisters' pants so they split open when she was on a date. And there was rolling my dad's car out of the driveway and down the street in the middle of the night with my girlfriends so we could take it without waking him up by starting the engine too close to home, and—"

Ad was grinning at her again by then. "You were *bad*."

"I spent a lot of time grounded," Kit said with a

laugh. Then, in her own defense, she added, "But I was on the receiving end of my sisters' antics plenty of times, too."

"You taught them well."

"I never get any sympathy," Kit pretended self-pity.

"So what did your mean sisters do to you?"

"It was my boyfriend who was lured away by one of my sisters. They put hot sauce in another boyfriend's iced tea and made it look like I'd done it. The puppy dog nose was retaliated for with permanent-marker freckles all over my face. For that chunk of hair I cut, I was pinned down while that sister shaved the entire side of my head. And that was only some of it."

"Your folks deserve all the ballroom dancing they want. They earned it," Ad concluded. "And you better watch out, my mother says when you have kids they pay you back by being worse than you ever were."

"My mother says the same thing. I'm thinking I should probably never have kids, just to be safe," she joked.

They'd reached the alley by then and neither of them said much as they walked down the cobbled lane to the stairs that led to their apartments.

It was very late and there was no question that the evening was at its close. That fact seemed to hang over them, sobering them from the fun they'd been having. Or at least that was how it felt to Kit.

They climbed the stairs at a slow—maybe reluc-tant—pace, and when they reached the landing, Kit said, "Well, thanks for walking me home."

"Sure," Ad responded, sounding slightly distracted.

Kit leaned her back against her door and said, "I never did hear if you won or lost your game tonight."

"We won. But only by one run. We're hurtin' without Cutty. He's our power-hitter."

Kit couldn't think of anything else to say to that. Besides, here they were, standing under the moonlight, face-to-face and not far apart, and sports was the last thing she wanted to discuss when she looked up into Ad's striking features.

Then he took on some of the burden of keeping this going himself. "So, next up is the bachelor party," Ad said. "And you know, since we crashed your shower tonight, you girls could crash our deal tomorrow night."

"Is that an invitation?" Kit asked, realizing that even in the dim light she could still see the vibrancy of his eyes.

"If I admitted that I could get drummed out of the boys club," he said in a voice that was deeper, softer than it had been a moment before. "I'm just saying we'd have it coming."

"Yes, you would," Kit agreed.

"And since I'm spending the day in Billings with Cutty to do some shopping for a gift for Kira, and the party is tomorrow night, the only way I'll see you is the way I saw you tonight."

Did that mean he *wanted* to see her? That was how it sounded. And it gave Kit a charge to believe it.

But charge or no charge—and in spite of wanting to see him, too—there wasn't much she could do to accomplish it. "Kira and I are having beauty night tomorrow night. At her house. While we watch the twins. Facials, manicures, pedicures, the works. That doesn't sound like anything that's going to turn into crashing a bachelor party. And even if we did, wouldn't we interrupt the girl coming out of the cake or something?"

Ad smiled a delicious sort of smile. "You could always wear the Viking-stripper bra again."

"Viking-stripper?"

"That's what it looked like." Ad grinned. "You know, I have too good a time when I'm with you."

"I doubt if you'll miss me when you're in the middle of a bachelor party," she said.

"I don't know…I might. But if you aren't going to come to that, don't you need to do something to the cake afterward or something?"

"I need to work on the cake again on Thursday night. Not tomorrow night, no."

"Damn, I just can't catch a break here."

"Sorry," she said as if she wasn't. Although she really was.

They seemed to run out of things to say then. But still neither of them made a move to go in. Instead they stayed standing there, looking at each other.

And even though she'd ended the last two nights thinking about Ad kissing her and then not having it happen, and she didn't want to fall into that trap again, the thought was in her mind anyway.

Just then Ad surprised her by leaning forward and kissing her a kiss that was soft and sweet and brief. Much too brief.

Leaving her looking up into his eyes again after only a moment.

"That was just to say thanks for saving me from Amanda Barnes tonight," he said by way of explaining the kiss.

Not knowing how to answer that, Kit did what he'd done to the other woman earlier in the evening, she merely raised her chin, wondering all the while if it was true that there hadn't been anything more to the kiss than appreciation.

But if it *was* true, then there was no reason to wait around for more. So Kit said, "Have a good time shopping and doing the whole bachelor-party thing."

Ad just nodded. Then he confirmed her suspicion that no more kissing was going to happen by taking the final steps to his own door, leaving Kit to unlock hers as they both said good-night and went in.

But whether the kiss had been only a show of gratitude or something more than that, the feel of his lips on hers stayed with her long after she was in the studio apartment.

And so did the race of her heart.

And it *was* racing.

More than it had in response to any other kiss she'd ever had.

Appreciative or not.

Chapter Five

Kit sat on the top of the toy box in the nursery of her best friend's new house the next night, watching Kira read a bedtime story to the adorable Mandy and Melanie. It was a warm, touching scene, and Kit was a little in awe of how Kira had adapted to the role of mother. And wife, too, for that matter, even though she wouldn't technically be Cutty's wife until the wedding on Saturday.

Her friend sat in a rocking chair with the babies on her lap, reading the tale of a bear lost in the woods. Kira was putting great drama into her rendition, doing different voices for all the characters, and making sure both curly-headed babies got to touch the bear's fur on each page.

The tiny girls were snuggled into her. Mandy was resting her head against Kira's chest. Mel was rubbing a fold of Kira's shirt between two pudgy fingers of one hand and sucking the middle fingers of her other hand. And it was obvious that Kira relished this end-of-the-day ritual.

It was nice, Kit thought. Nice to see Kira doing it all so well. Nice to see the babies responding to her as thoroughly as if she'd given birth to them. Nice that everything had worked out for Kira.

Kit was happy for her.

And maybe just a tad envious that her friend had been able to find a man to love the way Kira loved Cutty and would now have a life with him. It was something Kit hadn't been able to achieve for herself. Despite having tried. Twice.

"Say night-night to Kit," Kira instructed the twin girls after she'd read the last page, closed the book and set it aside.

"Ni-ni, Ki," Mandy said sweetly.

"No ni-ni," Mel refused firmly.

Kit had seen enough of the nineteen-month-old babies since arriving in Northbridge to know that Melanie was the more strong-willed of the two, and she tried not to laugh at the infant rebellion.

"Yes, night-night," Kira countered. "It's bedtime and you both have to go to sleep."

Mel's bottom lip shot out in a pretty pout and she pointed to the spot on her head where stitches proved she was also the more adventurous. "Boo-boo," she said as if that was going to get her the chance to stay up.

"Yes, you have a boo-boo. But you still have to go

to bed," Kira insisted, clearly working to suppress a smile. "Now say night-night to Kit."

Mel frowned at Kit but conceded, grumbling a petulant, "Ni-ni."

Kit had been in on the pre-bed routine enough times this week to play her own part and she knew that was her cue to abandon her perch on the toy box and cross to the rocking chair.

"Night-night, Mel," she said, bending to kiss the baby's chubby cheek before she took Mandy out of Kira's arms to help out.

Kit lifted the other twin into her crib as Kira stood to deposit Mel into hers.

"Night-night, Mandy," Kit repeated to her charge, accepting the puckered up kiss that the more affectionate Mandy craned upward to bestow on her lips.

Then Kit moved to the bottom of the side-by-side cribs so Kira could lie first one, then the other of the twins on their backs, cover them and kiss them good-night herself.

"Sleep tight, my beauties. I love you both," she said, turning off the lamp on their dresser as Kit stepped out into the hall.

"Ni-ni, Kiwa," Mel answered, already sounding half asleep and apparently having forgiven Kira for making her go to bed.

Kira said one more good-night, then joined Kit in the hallway, pulling the door partly closed after her.

"They're such sweethearts," Kit marveled.

"I know," Kira agreed with a note of maternal pride. "And you're so good with them."

"I'm still learning, but I'm getting better," Kira said as they went down the stairs.

They'd already done their facials—complete with mud masks, exfoliating scrubs and soothing toners, which Mandy and Mel had gotten into, too. To avoid the little girls playing with the nail polish, Kit and Kira had saved the manicure and pedicure for after the twins' bedtime.

"Let's refill the iced teas and get some cookies before we do nails," Kira suggested, passing through the living room to go to the kitchen.

Kit followed, saying as she did, "Who would have thought six months ago that you'd be getting married and adopting two babies?"

"I know. It's weird, isn't it? So much has changed in such a short time. My whole life."

"Are you okay with it all? No cold feet now that formalizing everything is getting closer?"

Kira made a face that let Kit know she was reluctant to give the answer she was about to give. "No, no cold feet. Sorry."

Kit knew what her friend was apologizing for but Kira qualified it anyway by adding, "But just because I don't have any doubts doesn't mean you were wrong because you did. In fact, if anything, the way I feel makes me all the more sure you did the right thing both times—I don't have a single hesitation. I can't wait to be Cutty's wife."

"And the thought of spending every day for the rest of your life with him?"

Kira pressed a hand to her heart. "It gives me this feeling of peace and contentment and just pure joy that tells me it's right. That everything about it is right."

"I'm glad for you," Kit admitted, suffering all the more envy in silence.

They poured and sweetened glasses of tea, grabbed a box of fancy chocolate-chip cookies and headed back to the living room.

"You seem to be fitting in to the whole town pretty well," Kit observed. "I was surprised by how friendly and laid-back all the shower guests were last night. They treated you as if they've known you all your life."

"They really have welcomed me as one of their own. It's like I've just come home."

Kit and Kira both sat on the sofa, setting down their glasses and the cookies, and reaching for the box that held all Kira's manicure supplies.

"I was a little drunk last night," Kira admitted, out of the blue. "It slipped my mind until now, but what was that whole thing with Amanda Barnes?"

Kit had been hoping that, since her friend hadn't brought it up all day and evening, Kira was going to let it slide.

"What whole thing?" Kit asked, playing dumb and keeping her fingers crossed that Kira was thinking of something else that involved the college secretary.

"That whole thing about how I don't do fix-ups," Kira explained.

So much for keeping her fingers crossed.

"And that lie you told about me arranging a bad blind date for you," Kira continued. "You didn't like the idea of Amanda going out with Ad, did you?"

Kira knew her too well.

But still Kit tried to cover her tracks.

"Ad says she's been stalking him since she moved to Northbridge and he doesn't like her."

"I haven't heard that."

"Ask him yourself if you don't believe me," Kit said defensively. Probably *too* defensively. But while she'd been inclined to talk things out with her friend, suddenly admitting to all that Ad raised in her—and having Kira encourage it the way Kit now knew Kira would—didn't seem like such a good idea. Denial seemed like the better route at that moment.

Unfortunately, denial didn't convince Kira.

"Well, maybe he doesn't like Amanda," Kira said. "But I had the distinct impression that *you* didn't want them getting together. That you were jealous."

"Me? Why would I be jealous? I've only known the guy a few days. He doesn't mean anything to me. Plus I'm taking a break from men. Not to mention that we live in different states and probably won't ever even see each other again after the wedding, and—"

"And you certainly do have a lot of reasons prepared. You've done a lot of thinking about it."

"They're all obvious reasons. I didn't have to think about it to come up with them."

"Uh-huh. Well, after the way you acted with Amanda I took another look at you and Ad when he got here. He headed straight for you the minute he could and stuck to you like glue from then on."

"I was running interference for him with Amanda Barnes because he asked me to. He owes me for it."

Kira laughed. "Uh-huh," she repeated sarcastically. "You also light up around him."

"I do not!"

"Oh, you do. You smile and laugh and don't even know there's anybody else in the room. And he's the same with you."

Kit rolled her eyes. "You're imagining things. You said yourself that you were a little drunk."

"I wasn't *that* drunk."

They both had foam spacers holding their toes apart by then and they chose different colors to paint their nails.

"So don't you want to know all about him?" Kira asked, as if she had top secret information that she knew Kit would want.

Kit realized that she should deny any interest at all if she was going to keep up the facade of indifference. But now that her friend had offered, it was difficult not to take the bait.

"What is there to know?" she asked with an effort to sound disinterested.

"That he's a great guy, for one," Kira said as she propped her feet on the edge of the coffee table and bent far forward to apply the polish. "Cutty says he couldn't have made it through Marla and Anthony's deaths without him."

Marla had been Cutty's first wife and Kira's stepsister, and Anthony had been Cutty and Marla's autistic son. Marla and Anthony had been hit by a truck and killed just after the twins were born.

"Cutty says," Kira continued, "that Ad kept him going. Above and beyond the call of duty—that's how Cutty put it. He says Ad saved his sanity."

Somehow none of that surprised Kit about Ad.

"He's wonderful with the girls, too," Kira went on. "I wouldn't expect a single guy to pay any attention to two babies, but he brings them toys and gets down on the floor to play with them. They love him. Plus there's his family—he makes sure his mother is taken care of, he's close to his brothers and his sister. He even vouched for his brother Ben at the bank when Ben wanted to buy the school for troubled kids outside of town."

"Ben is the bad boy everyone was talking about last night, right?" Kit said as she finished her right foot and switched to her left.

"Apparently he *was* a bad boy when he was a kid. But he's an adult now, and Ad believes what he went through himself has left him with a lot to offer kids who need help. Cutty says Ad stood by Ben when he got into trouble as a boy. That once or twice he even tried to take the blame for something his brother did to keep Ben out of trouble."

"So how has this amazing guy escaped the clutches of women like Amanda Barnes?" Kit asked, as if she thought her friend was exaggerating when, in fact, she didn't find any of what Kira said about Ad far-fetched.

"There *was* someone," Kira said. "But I haven't gotten the story on that yet. All I know is that it was rough on Ad. He wants to find someone else, though, to settle down with, get married, have a family."

"Then he's *really* not the man for me, is he?" Kit said somewhat under her breath but with a whole rash of sarcasm of her own.

"Come on," Kira cajoled. "You don't mean that. Just because things haven't worked out before—"

"It wasn't just that things didn't work out before, Kira, and you know it. You know it was me."

"You did what you needed to do."

"But didn't I just need to do it because I'm some kind of commitment-phobic nut-job who doesn't know a good thing when she has it? Twice?"

"That was Bert's mother talking. I hate that her nasty remark is what's stuck with you."

"Well, whether she was on the money about me or not, I don't think we want to take a guy like Ad and put him at risk with me."

Kira shrugged elaborately. "Okay, then I guess Amanda Barnes will just get him," she goaded.

Kit wasn't going to let her friend know just how much of a blow that struck so she pretended more indifference. "Good. I'll come back to town and do their wedding cake, too."

That made Kira laugh. "And then I'll visit you in jail when Cutty has to lock you up for poisoning the bride."

It was after midnight when Kit left Kira's house. If Cutty had come home before Kit was ready to leave, the plan was for him to stay with the twins while Kira drove Kit back to the apartment. But because he hadn't come home yet, Kira loaned Kit her car, instead.

Northbridge's streets were once again deserted as Kit maneuvered her friend's small sedan through them, and she was parking the car in the alley not ten minutes after pulling out of Kira's driveway. Since Cutty hadn't shown up at home Kit assumed the bachelor party was still going strong in the inner sanctum of the restaurant, and when she got out of the car not far from the kitchen door a wave of curiosity came over her.

What *did* go on at a bachelor party? she wondered.

It wasn't a question that had unduly troubled her in the past. But the fact that the party was underway just beyond that kitchen, set the wheels of her mind into motion. And once those wheels were in motion, it was difficult for her to simply walk by and ignore the opportunity to take a look for herself.

So, standing outside that door, she paused.

Should she? Should she sneak in the back door and play Peeping Tom on a bachelor party?

Probably not. It was an adolescent impulse, after all.

It reminded her of something she and a childhood friend had done the summer they were thirteen. They'd had crushes on the older boy who lived next door to Kit and every night, when his rock band had practiced in his basement, they'd belly-crawled like army guerrillas through the shadows to lie in the grass around the window well to watch him through the window.

But she was a long way from being thirteen now and

she should know better than to pull a dumb stunt like that. Yet she was still standing outside the kitchen door, unable to shake the urge.

She did have a sort-of-invitation, she reasoned. Hadn't Ad suggested the previous evening that since the men had crashed the shower, it would serve them right if the women invaded the bachelor party as payback?

Mmm. Maybe just a little look-see.

Fully aware that she shouldn't be doing it, she couldn't resist opening the door just a crack. Just far enough to get a glimpse of what was inside. A glimpse that would tell her if anyone was in the kitchen…

No one was.

That meant the coast was clear.

But what if she got caught? she asked herself, trying to challenge the urge that was getting stronger with every passing moment. What if she went in and peeked through the diamond-shaped window in the swinging door that connected the kitchen with the front of the restaurant, and someone spotted her with her nose pressed to the glass?

Now *that* would be embarrassing.

And anything that she knew from the get-go had the potential for embarrassment shouldn't be acted upon.

So close the door, climb the stairs and go to bed, she advised herself.

But still she didn't.

And the simple desire to be nosy wasn't the only thing that was keeping that door open. There was also the fact that if she did close the door and go up to bed, then an entire day would have passed without her even setting eyes on Ad.

That was really what was going on, wasn't it? she demanded of herself. She hadn't seen Ad since the night before and as curious as she was about what a bachelor party was like, what she really had up her sleeve was getting a look at Ad. And seeing what he was doing at the bachelor party. And if there were any unclothed or semi-unclothed women in there with him.

That was another reason why she shouldn't do it—she knew she should be fighting the attraction to him, fighting every urge, every impulse that had anything to do with him.

Yet she opened the door wide enough to slip into the brightly lit kitchen just the same.

So much for fighting urges and impulses.

On tiptoe, she scurried across the tiled floor to the swinging door.

She could hear music and boisterous male voices coming from the restaurant, but it was impossible to make out any of the words.

Somehow it seemed better that way, she decided, because taking one quick look at the event didn't seem quite as bad as eavesdropping on what was being said.

The problem was that when she got to the swinging door, she realized something that she hadn't noticed on the other occasions when she'd been in the kitchen—the diamond-shaped window was too high for her to see through.

But she'd come this far, she wasn't going to let a little thing like lack of height keep her from her goal.

She glanced around the kitchen for something she could stand on. There wasn't anything like a step stool that would have made it easy for her, but her gaze did light on a wooden, orange crate near the trash can, apparently waiting to be disposed of.

That seemed like a possibility, so she hurried to snatch it up and bring it back with her to the swinging door.

When she had it in place, she stepped onto it.

It gave her more elevation than she needed, and she didn't want to chance attracting too much attention so she kept her knees bent and slowly eased herself upward toward the window.

What she saw when she finally looked was unspectacular. There were no women—clothed or otherwise—and no giant cake for one to have come out of. There were just a bunch of guys, sitting around at the tables and at the bar where beer pitchers—some empty and some not—littered the surfaces.

Apparently toasts were being made because as Kit watched, beer mugs were held aloft and a cheer went up for something one of the men had just said.

"More talk than action," Kit muttered to herself as she scanned for Ad in the crowd.

He wasn't actually in the crowd, though. He was behind the bar, at the end that was just to the right of the door Kit was peering through.

Her heart started to beat double-time, both at her initial glimpse of him and at the sudden realization of how close by he was—close enough to see her if he just barely turned his head.

But even that fact wasn't enough for her to abort this foolish mission.

Instead, Kit stayed to check him out.

He had on khaki slacks and a plain white shirt with the sleeves rolled to his elbows—nothing remarkable— but still, to Kit, he was a sight for sore eyes. A sight she couldn't abandon even though she knew that the longer she stayed there, the more likely she was to be found out.

It was just that there he was, laughing and smiling. And when he did that those crinkles etched the corners of his eyes, and those sexy creases lined his cheeks. And she just couldn't make herself look away.

Until he glanced in the direction of the kitchen.

Then she ducked in a hurry, and the unthinkable happened.

The weight shift on the orange crate caused her foot to crash through a weak slat, costing her her balance, and down she went. With an involuntary shriek.

There was sudden silence in the restaurant.

As if it wasn't bad enough getting caught at what she was doing, now she was flat on her fanny on the floor with one foot wearing an orange crate.

Her impulse was to get out of there as fast as she could, so Kit yanked her foot out of the crate, leaped up and ran like mad for the door, charging through it just as she heard the swinging door bang against the abandoned orange crate.

She had no way of knowing if she'd made it outside

without being seen. But she didn't wait for Ad to widen his search to the alley and spot her there; she dashed up the steps, made quick work of unlocking the apartment door and rushed inside, closing the door behind her.

"I think you've gone out of your mind," she whispered to herself as she stood in the dark, hoping no one would ever know what she'd just done.

Not long after Kit had fled from the scene of what she considered her brief lapse in sanity she began to hear the bachelor party breaking up.

She'd spent the last few minutes pulling wood splinters out of her ankle and treating the scrapes. As a result, when she heard the knock on her door at 1:00 a.m. she was still dressed in the white shorts and pink T-shirt she'd had on all day, and she hadn't yet washed off her mascara or blush, or taken her hair down from where it was caught by a rubber band and left to explode in a geyser of curls at her crown.

So it wasn't her late-night appearance that caused her hesitation to answer her door.

It was the worry that Ad had come to confront her about the incident in the restaurant kitchen.

But if he knew that she had been the Peeping Tom he wasn't likely to forget about it, she lectured herself. And if she was going to have to answer for her actions sooner or later, she decided she might as well get it over with.

"Time to face the music," she muttered as she went to the door.

By the time she got there and opened it, though, no

one was standing on the other side. Instead Ad was sitting on the landing at the top of the stairs, his back braced against the railing, looking up at her with his aquamarine eyes reflecting the porch light.

"Come out and sit with me," he beckoned in that deep voice of his, not wasting it on a greeting.

"It's late," Kit responded, feeling much happier than she wanted to about seeing him, and knowing she should fight it.

"You're still up," he countered. "And dressed. So come out anyway."

He didn't sound drunk. But he did sound very, very relaxed. And appealing. And in spite of telling herself that appeal was all the more reason *not* to join him, Kit stepped onto the landing and pulled the door closed behind her.

His supple lips stretched into a lazy smile, and he patted the spot that was half-beside him, half in front of him. "Now sit with me."

Kit did that, too, settling into the narrow space left at the top of the stairs, ending up only inches away from him with her bare feet on the step just below.

Then she glanced at Ad and discovered that his smile had turned devilish.

His legs were bent at the knees and his arms rested on top of them with his hands dangling casually from there. But he raised one hand to point a long index finger at her scratched up ankle. "Are you okay?" he inquired.

From his position it would have been easy for him to see the scrapes, so that wasn't indicative of whether or not he knew she'd plunged her foot through the orange crate. And she wasn't about to admit to anything before she had to. So, with a glance at her abused ankle, she said, "It's nothing."

His smile grew broader still. And more devilish. "What about the rest of you? It sounded like you took a pretty good tumble in my kitchen."

So he did know.

But what was she going to say about it?

She didn't have the foggiest idea and while she was trying to come up with something, he said, "Don't deny it. I saw your head pop up in that window. And then I heard the crash."

He must have seen her before she'd realized he was near the door.

"I just wondered what went on at a bachelor party," she finally confessed with a plucky raise of her chin.

"You were too late for all the good parts," he said with an insinuative raise of one eyebrow.

"Really? What did I miss?"

"I'll never tell."

"Because there probably isn't anything *to* tell," she challenged.

"If you thought that you wouldn't have been standing on an orange crate to see for yourself."

She couldn't very well announce that wanting to see him had been an even bigger reason for what she'd done so she just let him believe that he was right.

"I'll tell you one thing, though," he said then. "If

you're thinking of changing careers, being a spy is not the job for you."

He'd enjoyed that because he was grinning as he laid his head back against one of the rungs of the railing.

"I guess I'll just have to stick with baking wedding cakes," she said, unable to suppress a smile of her own now that it was clear he wasn't angry or upset with her.

"Seriously," he said then, still not actually sounding it. "Did you get hurt?"

"A few splinters and some scratches when my foot went through the orange crate, and my pride is bruised, but otherwise, I'm unscathed."

"Anything I can do for your *pride?*" he asked, glancing at the part of her she was sitting on and letting more insinuation echo in his voice.

"I don't think so," Kit answered even as the very suggestion sent little shards of delight all through her. Then, to get the conversation off her mishap, she said, "Did you have a good time tonight?"

"I did," he said emphatically. "And it seemed like everyone else did, too. Although nobody would wear the Viking-stripper bra on their head, so maybe we didn't have quite as much fun as you did last night."

Oh, he was definitely feeling ornery. Kit just wished it didn't increase his charm quotient as much as it did.

"Maybe if you need a career change you could be that," he added as an afterthought.

"A Viking stripper?"

"Uh-huh."

"I don't think so," she repeated. "Besides, who says I need a career change? You haven't even tasted my cake and already you're condemning it?"

"Me?" he said in mock innocence. "I'm not condemning it. I'm just exploring your options."

Once more there was a lascivious undertone in his words.

Kit laughed and shook her head. "How drunk are you?" she asked when it occurred to her that he might be more than very, very relaxed after all.

"I couldn't drive," he confessed. "But I could probably stand on one foot, close my eyes and still touch my nose with my finger. Want to see?"

Okay, so maybe everything he said was going to sound deliciously sexy. "No, that's okay. I'll take your word for it."

"Good, because I was bluffing. If I stood on one foot I'd probably end up taking the same kind of header you did."

"That's getting old," she warned about the latest referral to her embarrassment tonight.

He grinned as if he was thrilled to have annoyed her. But he said, "Okay, I'll behave. We'll talk about something else."

"Good."

"So what *would* you do if you got sick of baking cakes?"

"Bake pies?" she joked.

"How 'bout doughnuts? Doughnuts are good. Northbridge doesn't have a doughnut shop."

"Oh, now I'm not only changing careers, I'm moving to Northbridge?"

"It's a nice place," he said as if he were trying to tempt her. "I know I'm never leaving here again."

He'd only alluded to having left the small town before but it was something Kit was curious about. And since he seemed more willing to get into it now than he had then, she said, "So you *haven't* always lived in Northbridge."

"Not always, no," he said. But his brows pulled together over the bridge of his nose in a frown that didn't infect the rest of his handsome face and he added, "But I feel too good to talk about *that.* Let's just say that I learned my lesson and made it my goal to find a nice Northbridge woman who wants nothing but to stay here, marry me, have my kids and make me doughnuts."

The nice Northbridge woman portion of that made Kit feel surprisingly dejected, but the mention of doughnuts again at the end left her laughing once more. "Wishing for doughnuts are you?"

"Something fierce," he confessed. Then, smiling at his own quip all the while still studying her, he said, "What about you, Ms. MacIntyre? Any nuptial plans on your agenda?"

"I've only had iced tea to drink tonight but I feel too good to talk about *that,*" she said forcefully.

"Hmm…" he mused, as if that made him suspicious. "So maybe you weren't joking last night when you said you're never going to have kids."

"Well, yes, last night I *was* joking. I like kids. I think, maybe, someday, I'd want to have a couple."

"Even if they turn out to be as bad as you were?"

"Even then."

"But without a loving husband?" Ad said, scandalized.

"No, there's a loving husband in the picture. It's just not a really clear picture, I guess. Certainly not as clear as yours."

He continued watching her, nodding his head as if she'd said something profound. "You just know you want to stay in Denver and go on baking wedding cakes," he said a bit sadly.

"Well, sure. That's where I live and what I do."

He went on nodding. And staring at her.

"What are you thinking? That that's bad?" she finally said, not completely understanding this conversation that seemed to have more importance to him than it did to her.

The nod switched direction and became a negative shake of Ad's head as he pushed away from the railing and sat up straight. "What I was thinking was that at least you're here now. And I'm glad."

So was she. Although she wasn't convinced that that really was what he'd been thinking.

She couldn't be overly concerned about it, however, because he was looking deeply into her eyes and the heat that his gaze seemed to emit wrapped around her and held her in a place that made everything else seem inconsequential.

Then he leaned forward and pressed his mouth to hers.

Somehow it didn't come as a surprise. It was as if his eyes had relayed the message that that was what he was going to do, and Kit merely closed hers and kissed him back.

Whatever he'd been drinking throughout the evening wasn't on his breath. He tasted sweet and clean and when his lips parted, Kit's did, too.

Yes, somewhere in the deepest recesses of her mind she realized that she was yet again doing exactly what she wasn't supposed to be doing, but she just didn't care. It was too nice to be there with Ad. To have him kissing her in a way that was different from the kiss of the previous night.

That first kiss had been more of a testing kiss. A kiss that had said he wasn't sure if he should. Or if she would let him. A kiss that had stopped short, as if to give them both the chance to reconsider.

But this kiss…

This kiss was more than that. It had familiarity. Confidence. The sense that it was precisely what he wanted and he wasn't going to beat around the bush about it.

And neither was Kit. She savored the smooth silk of his mouth; the faint brush of his breath on her cheek; even the slight, stubbled roughness of his beard against her skin—all the elements that made it a near-perfect kiss.

The only thing lacking was his arms around her. The feel of his hands, his touch. Her breasts in contact with his broad chest.

Realizing the direction in which her mind was wandering brought Kit up short. Ad might not be in complete control of his faculties, but she was. Or she was *supposed* to be, at any rate. And it was bad enough that they were kissing again, she certainly shouldn't be entertaining thoughts of it being even more involved.

She knew what she had to do. She had to put a stop to this.

It was just that she was enjoying it so much. Too much. Too much to let it go on, to let it go further.

So, reluctantly, she eased out of that kiss, pulling away from Ad. Then she opened her eyes and said, "You should probably sleep this off."

His eyes remained closed but he smiled a leisurely smile and fell back against the railing again. "That," he decreed, "does not sound like fun."

He was right, it certainly didn't sound like as much fun as what they'd just been doing. But still Kit held her ground. "I think you've had enough fun for one night."

"Not nearly," he disagreed.

But he finally opened his eyes to look at her again.

Then he sighed a deep sigh. "I have to move furniture for my mother tomorrow. I suppose I should rest up."

"You should."

He grinned incorrigibly. "Want to tuck me in?"

"Sorry," she said, as if it wasn't an intriguing idea.

"Me, too."

Kit got to her feet and held out a hand to help him to his. "I will make sure you can stand up without falling down these steps, though," she offered.

He grinned even wider. "Okay." Then he took her hand in his big, powerful one and the kid-leather feel of it sent shock waves up her arm in a way that she hadn't imagined when she'd wished for his touch moments earlier.

He stood without any problem at all, pulled her hand to his mouth and kissed the back of it.

"You're sure you're all right?" he asked when the brief, gallant buss was over and he'd let go of her.

"Positive," she said in a voice that came out soft and breathy and revealed the impact of his touch, his kiss, of him.

An impact she didn't want him to know about.

So she said a hurried good-night and made her second quick getaway into the apartment, leaving him standing out on the landing.

But still she brought a little of him with her.

Because that was when it occurred to her that while her fall from the orange crate honestly hadn't left any lingering effects beyond a few scratches, that kiss she'd just shared with Ad, and everything his touch had inspired in her, were hanging on with a life of their own.

Chapter Six

Ad wasn't surprised to see his brother Ben's car in the driveway of their family home when he arrived there himself Thursday afternoon. His mother had said she would see if she could get one of his brothers to come help move the living-room furniture, too. Ad hadn't expected that Ben's twin—Cassie—would come as well, but her car was in the driveway behind Ben's.

So Ad parked at the curb.

"Let me guess—" he said to his siblings in greeting after he went in the front door of the two-story, redbrick home with the wide front porch and found them standing in the living room "—Ben and I are just here for muscle, Cassie is here for decorating advice."

"And Mom is running late and isn't home at all," Cassie said. "She left a note telling us to wait for her."

"Cass and I were about to hit the fridge for iced tea," Ben added. "Want some?"

"Sounds good to me. It's nearly a hundred degrees out there."

The three of them filed through the living room into the big country kitchen in the rear of the house, talking about the high temperatures along the way.

But once they got there Cassie aimed a goad at her brothers. "I understand you boys did some heavy-duty partying last night."

"Cutty's bachelor party," Ad confirmed as he and Ben sat at the round pedestal table and let their sister do the work of getting iced tea for them all.

"Ben's been complaining of a hangover," the only Walker daughter said. "How about you, Addison?"

Ad glanced at Ben. "*Addison?* Am I in trouble for celebrating the last few days of my best friend's freedom?"

"Not that. Something else," Ben said, as if he were giving the information behind their sister's back even though she was near enough to hear him.

Cassie brought the iced teas to the table and took a seat for herself beside Ben and across from Ad.

With the exception of being the same age, Ben and Cassie didn't share any more than a general resemblance and the family coloring that all the Walkers had—dark, sable brown hair and blue-green eyes.

"What am I in trouble for?" Ad inquired of his sister, not taking it too much to heart because he couldn't think of anything he'd done wrong.

"Amanda Barnes," Cassie said.

"Ahh." Ad drank some tea, knowing that Amanda Barnes and his lack of interest in her was a sore subject with his sister.

"She called me and wanted to know what was up with you," Cassie continued. "Not only have you dodged everything I've tried to do to set up the two of you, but apparently you blew her off at Cutty's house the other night when you were together."

"He did," Ben confirmed, clearly enjoying the chance to stir things up in much the way they'd all liked to cause trouble with each other as kids.

"You know," Cassie chastised, "I have to work with Amanda."

Cassie was the counselor at Northbridge College where Amanda was a secretary.

"Oh, well, in that case, let me go ahead and just marry her to spare you the awkwardness of Amanda Barnes never taking a hint," Ad said facetiously.

"Okay, I'll call her back and tell her to buy a wedding dress," Cassie countered, echoing his tone.

"Can't we just drop the Amanda Barnes subject once and for all?" Ad asked.

"She likes you—there are worse things," Cassie insisted.

"I'm not so sure about that," Ad muttered more to himself than to her.

"Seriously," Cassie persisted, "she's a nice enough person. And she's attractive. You could do worse. At least give her a chance. Go out with her. Spend more than two minutes talking to her before you completely write her off. Then, if you really don't like her, *I'll* tell her you're not ready for a relationship and get her to give it a rest."

"Hmm, let me think about it," Ad said facetiously once again, pausing a moment for effect. Then, as if he'd come to a recent conclusion, he said, "Nope. Not gonna happen."

"Why not?" Cassie demanded.

"There's just no chemistry, Cass."

"I don't know, Ad," Ben put in. "You're hell-bent on finding yourself someone in Northbridge so you don't end up in the kind of mess you were in with Lynda and that narrows the field. It seems to me you can't afford to turn up your nose at a woman who's as hot for you as Amanda Barnes is."

That was more troublemaking on Ben's part. He knew very well how Ad felt about Amanda Barnes because Ad had told him more bluntly that he wasn't fond of the woman.

Ad glared at him. "I also can't make myself be attracted to someone I'm not attracted to just because she lives in town and it's convenient and she works with Cassie and won't let up on me."

"And then, too," Ben said as if he were adding to the list, smiling smugly all the while, "there's that friend of Kira's from Denver who you're really interested in."

"Kira's friend from Denver?" Cassie reiterated, obviously surprised to hear this.

Ben was only too happy to fill her in. "A bunch of us from the team went to Cutty's house after the game

Tuesday night and you should have seen Ad—he was like a heat-seeking missile when it came to her."

"Kit?" Cassie said. "I met Kit at the shower."

"That's the night," Ben said. "Where were you when we got there?"

"I had a headache and I left right after Kira opened gifts."

"Too bad," Ben said. "If you had stuck around you would have seen old Ad here get all googly-eyed over Kira's friend. And with Amanda doing her damnedest to corner him, too. But he passed her up, found the curly-headed woman and stuck with her the rest of the night. In fact, now that I think about it, I was one of the last to leave and Ad was still there. I'll bet he took her home since he has her staying in the apartment right next door."

Ad wasn't about to confirm that he'd taken Kit home. *"Googly-eyed?"* he repeated, as if that were the only part of what Ben had said that he'd heard. "What is *googly-eyed?"*

Ben didn't have the opportunity to define it before Cassie said, "Kit isn't your type."

"What's my *type?"*

"Tall, blond, blue-eyed—" Cassie began.

Ben cut in to lengthen the list, "Kind of stuck-up and self-centered. Someone who wants everything her own way—"

"Thought highly of Lynda, did you?" Ad said with a laugh.

"Just telling it like it is. Or was. Amanda Barnes sort of reminds me of Lynda, though."

"Good. Then that means I've learned my lesson," Ad said. Then, to Cassie, he added, "So you're trying to get me into trouble by fixing me up with another Lynda?"

"Amanda isn't like Lynda in anything but the tall, blond, blue-eyed part," Cassie insisted. "But she does live in Northbridge and wants to stay in Northbridge and get married and have a family—just like you."

"Still—let me say this one more time because it's important—there isn't any *chem-is-try*," Ad emphasized each syllable of the word to get it through to his sister.

"But there *is* chem-is-try with Kit," Cassie concluded, laughing at him and obviously finding this new twist very interesting.

"I didn't say that," Ad denied.

"No, Ben did."

"I didn't say *exactly* that," Ben said. "Although from the sidelines, it *looked* like there was chemistry. It looked like there was plenty of chemistry. Once he got himself hooked up with Kit at Cutty's place he didn't even know the rest of us were alive. He just sat with her like some contented cat, all smiles and talking real quiet to her and—"

"Will you knock it off?" Ad said to his brother.

"Why would I do that when I've got you on the hot seat?" Ben countered with a laugh.

"I liked Kit," Cassie contributed then, ignoring the exchange between her brothers and staying with the subject she was clearly more interested in. "She's nice and cute. And you have the whole restaurant-catering-food thing in common. It could work."

Ad shook his head as if he couldn't believe this conversation. "Yes, Kit's nice. And not hard on the eyes. And no chore to be around," he said. "But she's also here for this week and this week only. Then she's going back to Denver and that'll be it. Over and done with. So the fact that I hid behind her to escape Amanda Barnes the other night doesn't mean a thing."

Ad had gotten a little too vehement by the end, and Ben and Cassie both laughed at him.

"What do they say about those who protest too much?" Ben asked.

"Uh-huh," Cassie agreed with him.

But Ad finally decided that turnabout was fair play and, once he'd calmed his tone considerably, he said, "So, speaking of women, Ben, I understand Clair Cabot is coming back to town to walk you through things at the school and help get you recertified so you can open up."

That definitely sobered the younger Walker, who had enjoyed the company of another of Cassie's friends during a recent class reunion. But something had happened between them that he wasn't talking about, something that had left a sore spot with the younger brother.

"Yeah, so?" was all Ben would say in answer to Ad's goad.

"So maybe Cassie here can fix *you* up in the romance department."

"Think again," Ben said forcefully.

"You liked Clair at the reunion," Cassie said, taking the bait that Ad had thrown and switching her attention to her other brother's love life.

Satisfied—and relieved to have the focus off of

him—Ad sipped his tea and stayed out of the debate that he'd just instigated.

But not only didn't he participate, he was really only half listening, too. His thoughts were still on Kit, the way they had been every minute since he'd met her.

He was thinking about what he'd told Cassie about Kit—that she was nice, that she wasn't hard on the eyes, that it was no chore to be around her. And he was also thinking about what a vast understatement it had all been.

Because Kit was so much more. Kit was great. Beautiful. And he never had as much fun as he did when he was with her.

In fact, no other woman compared. Certainly he didn't want to be with any other woman, and he couldn't even think of a woman who could hold a candle to Kit.

But Kit was out-of-bounds, he reminded himself.

And even though he knew that was true, even though he accepted it, it still made things seem all mixed up.

Because he didn't want anything to do with Amanda Barnes—the woman in Northbridge who probably did fit all his qualifications.

But he wanted *everything* to do with the woman from Denver who fit none of them.

"I'm just going to stop down in the restaurant to make sure Ad remembers that I need to work on the cake later tonight, and then I'll be over," Kit said into the phone at six o'clock that evening.

Kira was on the other end of the line and assured her that there was no hurry. "We did so much running around today in this heat that I'm wiped out. Cutty is treating us to pizza so I don't have to cook. He's also making us strawberry daiquiris, and we're going to sit in the backyard in the shade to eat. So we'll just wait to order until you get here."

"That sounds terrific," Kit said, meaning it because they genuinely had had a long day and a few hours of regrouping before she had to put the wedding cake together was just what the doctor ordered.

"Why don't you ask Ad if he can ditch work and come, too?" Kira added.

She made it sound very casual but Kit suspected her friend was matchmaking.

Still, Kit hadn't seen Ad since the night before and in her heart of hearts she knew that stopping downstairs to talk to him about the cake was just a way of getting a moment with him before she left for the rest of the evening. And if she was angling for a moment with him herself, she could hardly fault her friend for a little angling on her behalf. Even if it did mean that Kira was ignoring her denials that she was interested in Ad.

"I'll relay the invitation," Kit told Kira.

They hung up then and Kit made a beeline for the full-length mirror in the bathroom.

In the process of running more wedding errands that afternoon, Mandy had spilled apple juice all over Kit. And while she could have changed into something of Kira's, a cool shower had sounded so appealing that she'd borrowed Kira's car again to make a pit stop at the apartment, instead.

Of course she hadn't needed to wash her hair, too, but she had. And when she'd chosen a clean outfit she hadn't been thinking about an evening with Kira and her family. She'd been thinking about the end of the night when she would use Ad's restaurant kitchen to put together the wedding cake.

Not that she'd picked out clothes that would be good to work in, because she hadn't. The tight, white scoop-neck, cap-sleeved T-shirt she had on would be ruined if she got any chocolate ganache on it.

And the gray shorts? They weren't as tight or as short as the shorts she'd worn at the start of the week, but what had really been on her mind when she'd picked them was the way Ad had looked at her legs when she'd worn those others…

"You should be ashamed of yourself," she told her reflection.

But she didn't spin away from the mirror and change. She just checked to make sure she didn't need another coat of mascara, that her blush was well blended, and that her hair—which she'd pulled up to the crown of her head both because it was cooler and to keep it contained when she was in the kitchen later tonight—still looked the way she wanted it to.

Then she applied a touch of lip gloss, slipped her feet into a pair of barely-there sandals and left the apartment.

The kitchen door was open to the alley when she descended the stairs and she went right in. The staff there seemed more harried than usual so she just said a general hello and asked where Ad was.

One of the chefs pointed a thumb over his shoulder in the direction of the dining room and went immediately back to the plate he was arranging rather than offering any small talk.

So Kit didn't bother anyone else and simply pushed through the swinging doors to go out front.

That was when she realized why the kitchen was in such a rush. The place was packed, every table and every bar stool was occupied, and every inch of standing room at the door was taken up by people waiting.

Kit scanned the crowd for Ad and spotted him behind the bar at the end opposite from where she was. He had on blue jeans that rode his derriere like a dream and another polo shirt with the restaurant's logo above the breast pocket—this one a teal green that was almost the same color as his eyes.

As usual, he looked good, even if he did seem to be operating at top speed.

For no apparent reason, he spotted her just then and in spite of obviously being under a lot of pressure, he smiled, handed a tray of drinks to the waitress on the other side of the bar and headed for Kit.

"Want a job?" he asked when he reached her end of the bar.

Before Kit could respond a waiter shouted an order for beers and, without taking his eyes off Kit, Ad grabbed three frosty mugs from below the bar and began to fill them from the tap.

"Wow, big business tonight," she said, moving out of the way of the doors to stand alongside the bar.

"It's the heat. Nobody wants to cook, everybody wants to be where it's air-conditioned," Ad explained as he set the filled mugs on a tray and slid it to the waiter. "That would be great except that two of my waitstaff called in sick."

Kit had assumed he was joking when he'd asked if she wanted a job, but now she wondered. "Were you serious? Do you need help?"

"Do I!" He gave her the once-over with a slightly longer pause at her legs before his gaze landed on her face again and he said, "But you look so nice you must have plans."

"Pizza in the shade of Kira's backyard," she said, weighing her options even as she did.

She could spend a nice, relaxing evening sipping a cool drink and eating gooey, cheesy pizza in the cool of her best friend's yard, watching the twins play and talking with Kira and Cutty.

Or she could run her tail off waiting tables in a crowded restaurant. With Ad.

"Kira and Cutty would probably like a night to themselves," she heard herself say even before she'd consciously made the decision. Or had the time to talk herself out of it. "Just let me give them a call to tell them to order the pizza without me and I'm yours."

Okay, probably not the best way to have put that, but it did elicit a broad, sexy grin from Ad.

He refrained from commenting, though, and instead said, "Really? You wouldn't mind?"

"I was going to make it an early night with them

anyway to get back here to work on the cake. I don't know if you remembered that I needed to do that tonight—"

"Remembering that is what got me out of bed this morning," he said with innuendo lacing his words and his crooked smile.

But Kit let that go without a remark or a comeback, and finished what she'd been about to say. "I could wait tables and then make the cake."

"I feel a little bad taking you up on it but not enough not to."

"Just let me call Kira and tell her I won't be coming, and find out what she wants to do with her car—I drove it home today because I thought I'd be bringing it right back."

"We could run it over there when things quiet down if she needs it first thing tomorrow," Ad offered.

Something about that *we* gave her a soft, warm feeling that had nothing to do with the heat wave that had hit today. But Kit told herself she was being silly.

"I'm betting Kira doesn't need the car tonight and I can keep it till I go over there tomorrow," Kit said. "Just let me give her a call."

Ad reached under the bar and produced a cordless phone for her to use. "I'll let everybody know we're getting some relief," he said, leaving her to make her call.

Which was what Kit did, keeping an eye on Ad the whole time and trying to tamp down the sense of exhilaration she felt at the change of plans for the evening.

After all, it was crazy to feel exhilarated over having

just passed up a lazy summer evening with friends, in favor of the hard work of waiting tables.

But even so the exhilaration was there to stay. And she knew why.

It was because even hard work had a unique appeal when she would be doing it side by side with Ad.

And that was a fact she was a little afraid to examine too closely.

The restaurant stayed busy until well after nine o'clock that night. When the crowd finally thinned out and became manageable without her help, Kit switched gears—and jobs—and went to work on Kira's wedding cake.

She spent the remainder of the evening fashioning flowers out of fondant; making ganache with imported chocolate and heavy cream; pureeing raspberries, sweetening them, adding a touch of raspberry liqueur and then thickening it all to a jamlike consistency; making white chocolate butter-cream frosting; and then assembling the towering cake.

Ad was still too busy himself to play assistant the way he had the night she'd baked the cakes originally, and although Kit didn't want to admit that she missed him, she did.

Not that he would have been any help or that she needed any, she just missed his company. And even though he seemed to make an inordinate number of trips to the kitchen, it wasn't compensation enough for not being alone with him in the kitchen or having him to talk to.

Midnight had come and gone before the restaurant was completely closed and the staff—all but the bartender—had gone home.

As Kit put the finishing touches on the cake, she could hear Ad saying good-night to the bartender and letting him out the front door. She hoped that meant that Ad would join her but she had no way of knowing if he still had things that had to be done out in the restaurant.

Apparently even if he did, he ignored them because only moments after she heard the outer door close, Ad came through the swinging door into the kitchen.

He stopped short just inside.

"That's incredible," he said when he caught sight of the cake.

Kit merely smiled as he moved to the worktable and walked all the way around it to get a closer and more complete look at her work.

There were four cakes in tiers stacked directly on top of each other, decreasing in size to leave the top cake considerably smaller than the bottom, and five cakes the size of the top tier surrounding the lowest layer. The creamy, white chocolate frosting covering each cake formed a flawless base beneath equally white, hand-made flowers that seemed to cascade from tier to tier, falling finally onto the single cakes below.

"I can't believe you did all this yourself. It's a masterpiece," Ad said when he'd made the full circle.

"Thanks."

"And you did it all without me," he added in mock astonishment.

"That's the hardest part to believe," Kit joked. "But I do need you to help me put it away—it'll take both of us to move it."

"At your service."

While Ad propped open the walk-in freezer door for them, Kit readied the cake to be transported. Then—together and very, very carefully—they carried it to where it would stay until the wedding.

Once it was safely out of harm's way in the freezer, Ad took another long look at it as if he couldn't believe his eyes before they returned to the worktable, which was laden with the bowls, tools and utensils that she'd used.

That was when Kit discovered that in spite of the number of hours she'd just worked, she wasn't in any hurry to get through the cleanup. Because the end of the cleanup put an end to the day, an end to being with Ad.

"I never had time to eat tonight, did you?" Ad asked as they gathered everything up and took it to the sink.

"No, I didn't," Kit admitted. She'd been too busy to even think about it before that.

"I just realized that I'm starved. Are you hungry?"

Now that she thought about it, she was. "I could definitely have a little something," she told him.

"Then why don't you do the dishes, and I'll rustle us up something for a late supper?"

"It's a deal."

The supper Ad rustled up for them was two sandwiches piled high with ham, turkey, swiss and provolone cheese, lettuce, tomato, pickle relish, slices of avocado, and what he claimed to be his secret ingredient—crushed potato chips.

He had the sandwiches wrapped in napkins when Kit was finished with the cleanup and he handed her two bottles of soda to go with them.

"What do you say we dine alfresco?" he suggested. "I need some fresh air."

"On the stairs like last night?" Kit asked.

"Sounds good to me."

To her, too, so she didn't complain. She just took the sodas and led the way out the alley door, letting Ad lock up behind her.

They climbed the steps and sat on the landing much as they had the previous night after the bachelor party— partly facing each other, separated by mere inches. Only tonight, for the first few minutes, they just relaxed and ate and washed the food down with sips of cola.

Not until the edge was off their appetites did Ad say, "I can't tell you how much I appreciate you pitching in tonight."

Kit had had a lot of time for her thoughts to wander as she'd put the cake together. Part of what they'd wandered to had been the conversation she and Ad had had on that same spot the previous night. So now, with that in mind, she used his expression of gratitude as a segue. "I was happy to do it. But my services don't come cheap."

"Really?" he said with an intrigued arch of one eyebrow.

He'd offered to pay her earlier but she'd rejected it

and even turned her tips over to the other waitstaff. So he had to know that he was going to have to ante up with something other than money.

"What's it going to cost me?" he asked.

"Information."

"About?"

Kit had eaten all she wanted of the sandwich and set the remnants aside. After a last drink of soda she gave Ad a cat-that-ate-the-canary smile and said, "Last night you said you were never leaving Northbridge *again*. But you didn't want to talk about it. I want to know what that meant."

Ad made a pained face. "That information is a high price for waiting a few tables."

"A *few* tables?" she challenged.

He smiled, finished his sandwich, too, and rested his back against the railing to study her from beneath half-lowered eyelids.

"Still," he said, obviously not willing to give in easily to her demand.

"Oh, I get it, you don't make good on your debts," she said, pretending to be sizing up his character when, in truth, she was merely enjoying the sight of him sitting so close in front of her, his broad shoulders easily spanning the gap between the railing posts; his biceps bulging from beneath the short sleeves of his shirt; one knee raised to brace a muscular forearm; his other leg stretched down the steps, long and thick-thighed; and the porch light gilding his strikingly handsome, clean-shaven face...

"You drive a hard bargain," he said, his expression letting her know he wasn't bearing a grudge for it.

Then he conceded.

"I lived in Los Angeles for about six months a year or so ago."

"The dyed-in-the-wool Northbridge boy moved to the big city?" Kit said. "Did you just get an urge to try out how the other half live or what?"

"No, I didn't want to go. I've never had the urge to *try out how the other half live.* I've always loved Northbridge."

"So why leave?"

Somewhere in the course of this Ad had become more serious, more tense, much less relaxed. And while Kit didn't want to be the cause of that, it made her all the more curious.

"I left because of a woman," he announced after a pause.

"Who?"

That probably qualified as prying. But the intense need to know, now that they'd begun, got the best of Kit.

Still, not wanting to seem *too* nosy, she added, "Or is this too big a deal for you to get into with the lowliest of your food servers?"

That made him smile again, albeit only a small one.

"You're a lot more than the lowliest of my food servers." And there seemed to be a lot more to that statement than simply answering her attempt to lighten the mood.

But without explaining it, he went on to address her *who* question. "The woman's name was—is—Lynda Madson, and I was engaged to her."

"Oh."

Not the most articulate response. But somehow Kit hadn't pictured him being seriously enough involved with anyone to have been engaged.

Still, this time he filled her in without prompting.

"Lynda came to Northbridge to open a bank here three years ago. She was an executive in the organization, and this branch was her baby. She was here nonstop for two months, putting in long hours, and by the time she was ready for dinner most nights, her choices were pizza delivery, the sandwich machine at the gas station, or Adz. So she showed up here more often than not, by herself. She'd sit at the bar. I'd usually be there tallying up the day's receipts, and we'd get to talking. We just hit it off."

It didn't make any sense to Kit but the idea of that other woman with Ad nearly knocked her flat with jealousy.

Maybe she *didn't* want to hear this….

But it was too late because now that Ad had started, he continued.

"Once the bank was up and running," he said, "Lynda went back where she'd come from—L.A. But by then we had something going and for the next year we did the long-distance thing—she'd come here, I'd go there, or we'd meet somewhere in the middle. And we talked on the phone so much I actually got calluses on my ears."

That made him smile but seeing what seemed like a fond bit of nostalgia didn't relieve any of Kit's jealousy.

"Then I asked her to marry me and she said yes," Ad continued. "But we decided we couldn't go on doing the relationship long-distance. My business was here and I didn't want to leave Northbridge, so her leaving L.A. seemed like the most logical choice."

Logical choice or not, that part of the memory tightened his features again.

"She got herself appointed the local branch president, which sounds good but in reality it was a pretty big step down for her. She did it, anyway, though, and moved to Northbridge."

Kit couldn't help squirming slightly at the images that fact inspired—images of the other woman with Ad around town, in the restaurant, maybe sitting right where she was sitting now…

But Ad didn't seem to notice her discomfort. Or maybe he just thought she was altering her position on the landing. Either way he went on with his account.

"I was thrilled," he confessed. "It was probably selfish as hell when she was giving up so much, but I was where I wanted to be, with the woman I was wild for. We were getting married. I thought everything in my life had fallen into place."

But the sarcasm that edged his tone warned that that wasn't the case.

"What happened?" Kit asked.

He shook his head as if he couldn't believe how naive he'd been. "Lynda hated it here," he said bluntly. "Maybe that should have been my first clue that I wasn't going to be up to her standards—that she thought the place I loved was boring and pedestrian and antiquated—but I didn't see it at the time. I just thought she was having trouble fitting in. But the thing was, she never really got involved with things here or made friends because she didn't put any effort into it."

"That almost sounds a little like sabotage—if she was serious about making a life here," Kit ventured.

"True. Especially when you factor in that she actually resisted the overtures of some of the women—even of my sister. And, as a result, she ended up pretty isolated. Plus she missed living in a city, missed the conveniences, the options, the faster pace. And it didn't help any that she'd taken a step down in the career she'd devoted herself to before she met me—there was more resentment about that than she let me know at the time. Both because she'd actually taken the demotion and because she'd done it just so I could work in a *restaurant*."

There was disdain in that word that must have been an echo of how his former fiancée had said it. But Ad didn't explain it.

"Anyway, every aspect of small-town life rubbed her wrong—the fact that people know each other's business, that she saw the same faces over and over again, that there were only so many places to go and things to do. She said Northbridge made her feel claustrophobic." Ad shrugged helplessly, "She just hated it here."

"So she left," Kit guessed.

"After about five months. And I went with her. Not realizing yet that Northbridge and small-town life weren't the only problems."

"But you didn't want to," she reminded him to keep things going.

"No, I didn't want to," he admitted. "But I loved Lynda and we were engaged, and I couldn't just call it quits. She'd given my lifestyle a shot. I thought it was only fair that I try hers out. So my brother, Ben, took over the restaurant and I went to L.A."

"What did you do for work?"

He made a face that let her know he hadn't particularly liked it, whatever it was.

"I managed a place there that had just opened up," he said. "It was a bar and dance club. A rooty-tooty joint."

"Rooty-tooty?" she repeated. "What does that mean?" Kit couldn't help smiling at that despite the fact that he'd made it sound like a jail sentence.

Her smile elicited one from him, and she was glad to see it. "You know—not just anybody could get in. There was a guy at the door who sized up the crowd in line out front every night and only the beautiful people and the celebrities made it past the velvet rope. There were VIP lounges and some big-time bands and groups that played. One write-up in an L.A. magazine called it *the* place to be and to be seen."

Kit couldn't imagine him even having a drink in the kind of place he was describing, let alone running it. There he was, tremendously handsome but clearly a laid-back, down-home kind of a guy. "So you were a hotshot," she teased.

"I was."

"But you didn't like it." Another guess, but one Kit felt confident with.

"As much as Lynda hated Northbridge, I hated that whole scene ten times more. And the rest of living in L.A., too. The traffic and the noise and the rushing around and the whole image-is-everything thing and—" He cut himself short. "I didn't like it so much that it got to where I felt like I had a gut full of clenched fists from the minute my eyes opened every morning until they closed again every night. It just wasn't me."

"But your fiancée was happy?"

He didn't answer that readily, as if he needed to choose his words before he could.

Then he said, "She wasn't ecstatic, no. I mean, yes, she was glad to be back in L.A., back to climbing the corporate ladder. And in some ways she was happy with me. I believe she loved me. But she didn't like that I worked in the *food service industry,* as she called it."

He'd used the same derisive tone on *food service* as he had earlier on *restaurant.*

"But you ran a trendy night spot, not a restaurant," Kit pointed out.

"Still, it was a bar and while she liked to eat out and go clubbing, she didn't want to be connected with the people who worked at the restaurants or clubs."

"Ah," Kit said, refraining from making the derogatory comment she was inclined to make about Lynda. Then, when she was sure she had enough control not to, she said, "What did she want you to do?"

"Anything where I worked nine-to-five in a suit and tie."

"So you were supposed to give up your life here, move to L.A., and change a whole lot about yourself, too?"

Okay, so that had sounded sort of catty. But Kit couldn't help it.

Ad chuckled wryly. "Basically. But Lynda moving here and being a bank president rather than a corporate muckety-muck didn't do it for her, and me living in Los Angeles and being some kind of...I don't know what, didn't do it for me, so..."

He went from looking at Kit to gazing down the alley, and she could tell that coming to the conclusions he'd had to come to and accepting them had not been easy for him.

Kit didn't say anything. She let him have his moment and simply waited until he was ready to go on.

When he was, he turned his handsome face to her again. "Anyway, we just had to admit that we didn't have a future together. We wanted different things, different lives. And we couldn't get around it. So we said goodbye and I came home."

Kit could tell how difficult that had been just by the way he said it and her heart ached for him. "I'm sorry," she said softly.

"I was, too," he countered but with a small, one-sided smile.

"*Was?* Past tense?"

He nodded. "I took from the experience what I think I was supposed to learn from it and counted myself lucky that I wasn't in any deeper before I figured everything out."

"What lessons did you take from the experience?"

That was probably more prying but he didn't seem reluctant to talk about this anymore so maybe it wasn't so bad.

"I learned to take more into consideration when I meet someone I like."

"For instance?"

"Well, location is important to me. I never wanted to live anywhere but Northbridge before, but after my stint in L.A. that was cemented for me. I certainly don't want to get involved with anyone who's ashamed of what I do for a living, either."

"That's what you *don't* want. What *do* you want?"

"Someone pretty traditional, I guess. A little old-fashioned, maybe. Someone who wants to settle down, get married and stay married for the rest of our lives, have kids, grandkids, great-grandkids. I want someone who can find pleasure in small, simple things. Someone who doesn't need or want a lot of trappings."

"And all in Northbridge," Kit added for him.

"All in Northbridge. So now you're thinking I'm just a big hick, right?"

Actually, she was thinking that it all sounded good. And more appealing than it should. But that isn't what she said.

"I was thinking how nice it is that you know what you want and what you don't want," she said.

"Why? Don't you know what you want and what you don't want?" he asked, his eyes probing for the truth.

Kit laughed a little wryly. "I think I do and then I'm

not so sure, and then…" It was her turn to shrug. "Well, then things fall apart."

"Huh?" he said with a laugh of his own.

"Exactly—it's confusing. But it's too late tonight to try to understand."

"Not fair!" he said as if a referee had just made a bad call. "I told you my story and now you're going to leave me hanging?"

Kit smiled an evil-villainess smile. "I am."

Ad laughed and in that instant all the tension that had been in him seemed to evaporate.

"See? This is what I'm talking about—you big city girls just drive me crazy."

"I'll send word to Amanda Barnes that you're ready for her, then," Kit goaded.

He laughed even harder at that. "Bad to the core!" he said, reaching a playful hand to the back of her neck as if to force her to behave.

But the same way laughter had dissipated all the tension in the air, the moment his hand came into contact with the bare skin of her nape, playfulness turned to something else.

The strength Kit felt in that hand suddenly turned to tenderness as his fingers massaged and caressed. And just as suddenly his eyes seemed to delve into hers and offer the depths of his own in return.

"Oh, yeah," he said so quietly it was almost a whisper, "you city girls definitely drive me crazy."

He used the caress of her neck to pull her toward him as he leaned forward, kissing her. But while tonight's kiss was similar to the past night's kiss in the beginning, that was only true for a short while before it changed. Before his lips parted over hers and waited patiently for hers to part, too. Before his tongue came to introduce itself to hers. Before his arms wrapped around her to bring her closer still, and his hands pressed against her back to send a warm rush all through her.

No, when it came to relationships, she wasn't sure what she wanted. And he was. And she wasn't it. But at that moment none of that really registered as important in Kit's mind. At that moment, she was just lost in that kiss. Every sense was awakened by that kiss. And that kiss was turning her to jelly.

Kit took Ad's lead, meeting his tongue, matching it, toying and teasing and trading secrets. She raised her hands to his chest, letting her palms ride the hard mounds of muscular pectorals hidden behind his shirt, feeling the almost-electric energy that seemed to be shooting between them.

Her nipples hardened with the yearning for attention as her entire body came alive with new desires, new cravings. Cravings for the feel of his hands on more than her back. For the feel of his mouth, his tongue on so many more places than they were now.

Mouths were open wide by then, tongues were bold and demanding, and those demands seemed to reverberate all through Kit with a resonance that was increasingly difficult to ignore.

Except that just as she was thinking about meeting some of those demands, her mind took an unexpected turn and she found herself recalling all Ad had told her.

All he'd told her about what he wanted and how strongly he wanted it, how sincerely he wanted it. And she found herself recalling how free of doubts he was.

It was that kind of certainty that gave her pause. That kind of certainty in comparison with her own history. Her own completely different history.

And instead of letting her hands travel beyond his chest to explore other parts of him the way they were inclined to do, she used them to push him back just enough to end the kiss.

"Big city girl, remember?" she said, reidentifying herself in a breathless voice tinged with just how much she didn't want to be reminding him of that.

Ad took a deep breath and sighed it out long and slow. "They seem to be my weakness," he said then.

But he didn't try to kiss her again. He took his arms from around her and fell back to rest against the railing once more to look at her the way he had been earlier— very intently.

And between the heat that seemed to emanate from his eyes and the sight of those big shoulders and that massive chest she'd just moments earlier had her hands on, Kit knew she needed to do more than simply end a kiss or she was likely to be right back there, in his arms, clinging to his mouth with her own, letting her hands have their way after all.

"I think I better go in," she said weakly.

Ad didn't respond to that for what seemed like a long time. He merely went on studying her, bathing her in a look that made her want to stay and bask.

But then he nodded his head ever so slightly in agreement and that was the impetus she needed to get to her feet.

"Thanks again for your help tonight," he said softly as she unlocked the door to the studio apartment.

"Sure," she answered.

And that was how she left him, without a backward glance or even a good-night, before she went inside and closed the door.

Because the farther she'd gotten away from him, the more she'd known that she didn't want to go. That she wanted to turn around and leap back into his arms.

And one more glance, one more word, might have made her do just that.

Chapter Seven

The wedding rehearsal went smoothly Friday evening and then the wedding party headed for Ad's restaurant.

Ad had closed the place for the night, and the wives of Cutty's fellow police officers and several other Northbridge women had volunteered to prepare the buffet dinner.

Kit, Ad, Kira and Cutty were the first to arrive after the rehearsal and they were all surprised to find that the dining room had been decorated with an abundance of flowers and that candles had been placed on every table, lining the bar and any other surface that would hold them safely, to illuminate the space in a soft, romantic, golden glow.

Seeing it made Kira cry.

"Oh, Kira, this is a nice thing," Kit said to comfort her friend.

"I know," Kira wailed as the tears streamed down her face and both men looked on helplessly.

Other members of the wedding party came in then and although it didn't stop Kira from crying, it did make her grab Kit's arm in a panic. "Take me up to your apartment before anybody sees me like this."

"Okay, come on."

Kit quickly ushered Kira into the kitchen but that was a tactical error because the women responsible for the dinner and decorations were there getting ready to set out the food.

Thinking fast, Kit put herself between Kira and the women, draped an arm around Kira's shoulders as if to guide her and said, "Something just flew into her eye and I have to help her get it out," as she took Kira through the alley door before anyone had a chance to delay them.

Kit had a hunch why Kira had become so emotional over what they'd found in the restaurant, but not until she and Kira were in the studio apartment and Kira was dry-eyed again, did she say anything.

When Kira had recovered, Kit brought her a glass of water and said, "I know that when it came to Cutty, one of the biggest obstacles for you was that you were afraid that the people around here would never accept you. All those flowers and candles makes it look like you're getting the seal of approval, doesn't it?"

Kira nodded and drank some of the water.

She'd come to Northbridge in search of her stepsister and the son Marla and Cutty had had after Marla had gotten pregnant in high school and they'd eloped. Before the elopement, Kira had lived in her stepsister's shadow. When she'd discovered that Marla and Anthony had both been killed and she subsequently had stayed to help Cutty recover from his broken ankle and to get to know the twins, Kira also had found that Marla was admired, verging on adored by the people who knew her here. Kira had been very worried that she wouldn't be able to fill those shoes or live up to her sister's legacy. She'd been terrified that she would be met with resentment for even trying, and for ending up with her late sister's husband.

"The flowers and the candles were like a sign that it's okay that I'm marrying Cutty," Kira said.

Kit gave her friend a hug. "Of course it's okay that you're marrying Cutty," she assured. "No one can look at the two of you together and not know that you're good for each other. That you make him happy."

"All I know is that lately I've noticed that the comparisons to Marla have stopped," Kira said. "I'm not hearing her name every time I talk to someone, and nobody is telling me how Marla would have done this or handled that anymore. But I wasn't sure if that meant anything or not. I mean, the people here have been friendly to me right from the start. And warm and open. But I knew that could have been as much because I'm Marla's sister as because of me."

"I don't think those women downstairs would have gone to all the trouble they did if they weren't doing it for you, just because you are you," Kit said. "They weren't doing it for Marla and they had to know that Cutty—or any guy for that matter—wouldn't even notice that they'd gone the extra mile to make it so special. Or that Cutty or any guy would care much one way or another. I know they did it for you."

"I think so, too," Kira agreed, fighting not to start crying all over again. Then she managed a laugh through her almost-tears. "This is awful—here I am at my rehearsal dinner blubbering like a baby."

"No, you're not. You're getting something out of your eye," Kit joked.

Kira hadn't set her purse down in the restaurant so she still had it with her. Now she got up from the chair she was sitting in and took it to the mirror in the bathroom. "I better patch this mess I've made of my face," she said.

Kit laughed. "It is pretty bad—you look like a raccoon."

She went into the bathroom, too, wanting to make sure her own mascara and blush didn't need freshening.

"Did I tell you how much I like that skirt and top?" Kira asked then.

Kit glanced down at her outfit. She'd bought it especially for the rehearsal dinner—it was a dark navy blue, matte jersey-knit skirt that flowed over her curves like water and flared slightly around the bottom, and a matching square-cut top that fell to an inch below her waist from thin spaghetti straps.

"It's so comfortable you wouldn't believe it," Kit said. She'd caught only the sides of her hair up into a comb at her crown and left the rest in a riotous mass of curls, so while she was in the bathroom, she used the opportunity to brush the part that was free.

By the time she had, Kira had fixed the damages to her own face and was ready to go.

"No more tears?" Kit asked.

"I hope not. But stay with me while I thank everyone for what they did—maybe some moral support will keep me from crying while I tell them how nice I think they all are."

"I can do that," Kit said.

But she wasn't too sure if her friend was really going to be able to get through it minus tears when she could already hear the emotions building in Kira's voice as they went to the door and Kira said, "This little town really is a wonderful place. The only thing that would make it better for me is if you were here."

Kit linked her arm through her friend's. "I'm here now," she reminded.

"I know, but it would be so great if you *lived* here. You could marry Ad, and I'd be married to Cutty, and we could be neighbors and have kids together and—"

"You already have my husband picked out?" Kit asked with a laugh.

"I thought you could use a little help," Kira countered.

Kit didn't argue with that. But she did think that the help she needed was help staying away from Ad, not help hooking up with him.

Because hooking up with him was something she kept doing just fine on her own.

It was the staying away part she couldn't seem to stick to.

And since she had no intention whatsoever of making Northbridge her home, she knew she really, really should do that....

Kira didn't make it through thanking the women in the kitchen without tearing up again. But by the time she was finished telling them how much their kindness and thoughtfulness meant to her, everyone was a little soggy, including Kit.

Tissues were passed around and eyes dabbed at, but Kit was just glad to see that her theory had been right—Kira was not only being accepted in the place where she'd opted to make her life, but welcomed to it.

Then the women doing the dinner insisted that the bride-to-be go out into the dining room and enjoy herself, and Kit made sure Kira complied.

Professional caterers couldn't have done a better job with the food, and it was clear that as much extra time and effort had been put into that as had been put into decorating the restaurant. Beer and wine flowed freely—compliments of Ad—and the entire evening was a wonderful kickoff to the formal celebrations of Kira and Cutty's wedding.

As she had throughout the week, Kit enjoyed herself. Northbridge honestly did sport some of the friendliest, kindest, warmest people she'd ever met. But—also as had been the case all week—it was Ad who persistently caught her eye, her attention, her thoughts.

He was more dressed up than she'd seen him since she'd met him. He had on a pair of gray slacks that couldn't possibly have fit any better. Granted, his derriere didn't need much assistance—it was pretty amazing on its own—but in those pants! Kit could hardly keep from staring.

The darker gray shirt he wore with the pants draped across his broad shoulders and followed the line of the sharp V of his torso in its own version of perfection. But for some reason the part Kit liked best about it was the fact that he'd rolled the long sleeves up to just below his elbows, exposing thick forearms and wrists that her gaze kept snagging on almost as much as it did on his backside.

Plus he was clean-shaven and smelled of that signature cologne, and he'd had a haircut that had only barely trimmed his short-on-the-sides, mussed-on-top style. All in all, he just looked great. And so, so sexy...

Which was all the more reason, Kit told herself, why she should stay as far away from him as possible.

But that didn't work out since Ad spent the evening being so attentive to her that it was as if she were his date.

Of course she didn't exactly run from him. In fact, even though she knew she was just asking for trouble, the fact that they were basically coupled-up together gave her a tiny thrill. And on the rare occasions when she found herself without him, she missed him and couldn't help scanning the restaurant until she knew where he was.

That sense that they were a couple lasted throughout

the party and grew stronger still as Kira and Cutty left at the end of the night, after everyone else had gone. There was just something very couple-ish about Kit and Ad walking them to the door, standing next to each other as the four of them sorted through the details of the schedule for the actual wedding day.

Couple-ish enough for Kit and Ad to be standing close together. So close that their hands accidentally brushed.

And it *was* an accident, Kit was sure of it. It was just that rather than pulling his hand away when it happened, Ad took her hand in his, slipping his fingers around hers and into her palm to squeeze slightly before he let go.

It was no big deal.

Or at least that was what Kit worked to make herself believe. But believing that intimate, secret squeeze of her hand was no big deal was complicated when it felt very sensuous. And when it started a warmth that sluiced up her arm and spread all through her body, awakening something inside her that made her knees go weak.

"You're going to make it tomorrow, right?" Cutty asked.

"Make it?" Kit echoed a bit dimly, unsure what he was talking about and hoping that preoccupation hadn't caused her to miss something in the conversation.

"You'll show up for the wedding and once you're there you won't climb out the bathroom window and take my bride with you," Cutty explained.

He was only good-naturedly teasing her but Kit wished he wouldn't have said that.

Still, she put some effort into being a good sport about it. "I'll be there," she said, pretending not to notice the curious glance Ad cast her way. "And so will Kira," Kit added. "Unless she changes her mind."

Kira laughed. "Not a chance." Then, with a playful elbow-jab at Cutty's ribs she said, "You weren't supposed to bring that up again."

"Oops," Cutty said, making an I-shouldn't-have-opened-my-mouth face, "I forgot."

"We better go before you forget anything else," Kira said. "We'll see you guys tomorrow."

Kira and Cutty thanked Ad for everything and they all exchanged goodbyes before Kira tugged Cutty outside.

"Climbing out a bathroom window?" Ad repeated the minute he had the door closed and locked behind them.

Obviously that was as long as he could contain his curiosity.

But Kit ignored the query and instead made a show of looking around at the coffee cups, glasses and dessert dishes that were all that remained of the rehearsal dinner after the makeshift kitchen crew had cleaned the dinner debris.

"Let me help you clean up the rest of this mess," she said rather than addressing Ad's question.

Then she moved back into the center of the dining room where the dinner had been held.

In order for the entire wedding party to sit together tonight, several tables had been pushed together. Kit left them that way and began to gather dishes, cups and glasses into stacks.

Ad joined her but he didn't go to work. He stood nearby and, even though Kit didn't look at him, she could feel his gaze on her.

"Does the bathroom-window thing go along with the wedding-willies comment Cutty made a few nights ago?" Ad asked.

"You don't really want to hear about it," Kit said as if it were nothing.

"What if I do?"

"You don't," she said breezily. Then, changing the subject, she said, "We need a bus tub. I'll go get one."

And she left him behind, disappearing into the kitchen.

When she got back, Ad was standing in the same spot he had been, waiting for her, watching her every step of the way as she rejoined him at the side of the table.

But Kit went about her business as if she weren't under his scrutiny. She set the gray plastic caddy in the center of the tables that had been pushed together and started filling it with the dirty dinnerware.

After another moment of just studying her, Ad began to help. But he still didn't let her off the hook.

"Last night when we were talking about my relationship with Lynda you said it was nice that I know what I want and what I don't want. You also said that you think you do and then aren't sure, and that then things fall apart."

Maybe it wasn't such a good thing when a man listened closely enough to what was said to remember it, Kit thought.

"Did I say that?" she hedged.

"You did. And I can't help wondering if the wedding-willies comment and this climbing out the bathroom-window deal are connected."

"You're wondering that, are you?"

"Uh-huh, I am."

"Well, it's late. It's almost eleven."

"That's not so late."

Still, Kit didn't address that and instead said, "Why don't I take these in and get them into the dishwasher? And while I do that you can wipe off the tables and put them back where they belong?"

Ad didn't say anything.

Wondering why, Kit finally cast a glance at him.

He was smiling a small, lazy smile, clearly amused by her hesitation and all her dodges.

Then, he said, "It's only fair that you tell me your story. Besides, I'm beginning to think yours might be more interesting than mine."

The smile notwithstanding, Kit still wasn't eager to tell him what he wanted to know, so she said, "Don't be too sure," picked up the bus tub and brought it with her to the kitchen.

She didn't expect Ad to take her suggestion and re-arrange the dining room. She thought he would follow her and persist in his quest for answers.

But he didn't.

And it gave her time to consider whether or not she was going to talk about what she considered her check-ered history.

Of course if she *didn't* tell Ad about it he could probably find out from Cutty anyway. She was sure all he had to do was ask.

So why hadn't he? Especially after the wedding-willies comment earlier in the week.

Maybe because he hadn't been inclined to pump his friend for dirt on her? Maybe because he'd respected her privacy enough to wait for her to tell him about herself? Maybe because he hadn't wanted to enlist his friend to gossip about her behind her back?

Those were all nice reasons. And, thinking about the sort of man Ad was, she had no problem believing that they were true.

Maybe he deserved to be rewarded by having his curiosity satisfied, the way he'd satisfied hers the night before.

"Are you still in there?" he called from the dining room.

"Yes," she called in return, not yet sure whether to tell him about her greatest embarrassments or not.

"Well, come back. If you really don't want to talk about your sordid past we don't have to."

That made her laugh. "Who said it was sordid?" she shouted.

"I'm just figuring…"

She was still smiling and suddenly the idea of being open and honest with him didn't seem quite as daunting as it had.

So maybe she should tell him, she thought as she closed the dishwasher and dried her hands.

"Whatever you do," he called again, "don't go out a window. I don't know if I'm insured for that."

Okay, she was going to tell him, she decided after laughing again at his joke.

She turned back toward the door that connected the dining room. But still, talking about her former relationships wasn't an easy thing for her to do and she realized that she had butterflies in her stomach at the prospect.

"Here goes," she muttered to herself, hanging on to her resolve as she headed in that direction.

Ad had all the tables where they belonged when Kit rejoined him. He was behind the bar, putting away the rag and spray bottle he'd used to clean them.

His remarkable eyes raised to her the moment she entered the dining room and this time when he smiled at her it was more indulgent.

"Relax," he advised. "We can talk about the weather or world events."

Once more he made Kit smile even as she considered not going through with this after all.

But it was almost as if she wanted to confide in him now. For no reason she understood. Except possibly that the man always seemed to make her feel better about herself and everything else, and maybe she was hoping he could take this and put a more positive spin on it.

"No, it's okay," she informed him. "I'll tell you about my *sordid* past. But I'm warning you, it's not a pretty story."

"Oh, good. Those are my favorite kind."

"Sure, you say that now, but in the end you could be sorry."

He grinned. "This just sounds better and better."

"And you might want to kick me out of your apartment in the name of your fellow men and never see me again."

His eyebrows arched. "What are you? The Black Widow killer?"

"Not quite. But close," she joked.

Ad stayed behind the bar and Kit went around to the front of it, sitting on one of the stools across from him.

The place was still lit only by the candles everywhere, the scent of flowers lingered in the air, and it struck her that this was far too romantic a setting to say what she was about to say.

"Maybe we should blow out the candles and turn on the house lights," she suggested.

"And should I get a kitchen knife for protection in case you go wacko on me?"

"Okay, okay, it's not *that* bad."

"Then let's leave the candles. I kind of like them." The innuendo in his tone let her know that he really wasn't taking any of this seriously, which helped ease some of her own tension.

Still, though, she couldn't look him in the eye so she took a plastic, sword-shaped toothpick from a container on the bar and began to fiddle with it, keeping her gaze on that, instead.

"I've been engaged twice," she finally announced.

"Really?"

"Even if it surprises you, you should try to hide it," she advised.

"Sorry. It was the twice part that took me off guard. Engaged, but not married?"

"Engaged but not married. Never married."

"Because you're afraid of weddings?" he guessed, clearly connecting the wedding-willies comments to this.

"No, not because I'm afraid of weddings. It isn't as if I freak out over going to someone else's wedding. Cutty was only teasing about that. It's just that I haven't made it to either of my own."

"You just like getting engaged?" Ad asked with a gentle levity to his voice.

"It's not like I go out beating the bushes for it, no. Both times it came in the normal course of events. Bert and I had dated for almost two years, and I'd been with Tim for over a year."

"And you accepted their proposals because you loved them?" he prompted.

"I thought I did. But then…I guess I didn't love them enough."

Ad nodded. "Yeah, I wondered about that with myself and Lynda, too—if maybe, even though I thought I loved her an amazing amount, it just wasn't enough," he admitted. "So how close did you come to marrying these guys?"

She knew he was thinking about Cutty's climbing-out-the-bathroom-window remark.

"That's been the problem. I mean, if I'd broken off the engagements early on, it wouldn't have caused such a mess. But both times I got pretty close," Kit said ominously.

"How close?"

"The first time, I was within twenty-four hours of the ceremony. We'd already had the rehearsal dinner and everything."

"And the second time?"

Kit grimaced. "Out the bathroom window at the church fifteen minutes before I was supposed to walk down the aisle."

Ad didn't say anything to that and a curiosity of her own made her take a surreptitious glance at him from beneath half-lowered eyelids.

He was struggling not to laugh.

That eased more of her tension. At least he wasn't horrified.

"You think it's funny?" she asked.

"I'm sorry. I'm sure it wasn't funny to the guys and I'm figuring you didn't do it lightly either time. It's just that I keep picturing you—decked out in the big white dress and veil—climbing out a bathroom window. Then what did you do? Catch a bus home?"

"Kira came with me and we took her car."

That made him laugh out loud. "Kira went with you?"

"She was my maid of honor and when she came looking for me and found me going out the window…" Kit shrugged "…she came, too. She's a good friend."

"No wonder Cutty is worried about you going out a window tomorrow and taking her with you. There's a precedent for it."

"It's not like I'd kidnap her from her own wedding. But if she decides fifteen minutes before the ceremony that she wants out—I'm with her. I owe her."

Again from under her half-mast eyelids Kit saw Ad struggling to contain his amusement.

When he had, he said, "Okay, if it wasn't the weddings themselves that sent you running, what was it?"

Kit's embarrassment increased a notch and she twirled the sword-shaped toothpick more furiously.

"There weren't big reasons either time," she admitted. "That's the problem. There I was—twice—with a lot of time and money spent, and people invested in the idea that I was getting married, and yet I bailed for what almost everyone thought were petty reasons since it wasn't as if I caught either Tim or Bert cheating on me or found out they were compulsive gamblers or had criminal records or something. It was just that the closer the weddings got, the more I started to think that I couldn't handle certain things about them. Not when it was going to be for the rest of my life."

"Like what? One of them ate crackers in bed and the other one was a nose-picker?"

Kit smiled again at his joke. "With Bert—that was wedding number one from three years ago, just after I'd become good friends with Kira—it was the fact that everything had to be regimented. We had to have meals at exactly the same time every day. Towels had to be folded a certain way. Canned goods had to be lined up perfectly and alphabetized on the shelves—"

"Alphabetized?"

"He liked everything neat and tidy and well-organized."

"Alphabetized canned goods is beyond well-organized. I thought that was just a gag they used on sitcoms. I didn't think anybody actually did it."

"Bert did."

"What happened if you put corn before beans?"

"He got very upset when anything was out of order— if the throw pillows weren't precisely placed, if his toothbrush wasn't facing the right way—he said it knocked him off-kilter for days."

"Ah," Ad said as if he didn't know what else to say. "And what about the other guy?"

"Tim. That wedding was about seven months ago. He was completely different from Bert, which to me seemed like a reason not to worry—"

"Until fifteen minutes before the ceremony," Ad reminded.

"Well, I had started to worry before that, but I kept telling myself Tim was easygoing, he didn't care about the things Bert had been obsessed with, so it would be okay. Anyway, Tim thought he was some kind of super-star—in fact, he would literally tell me that. And that it was frustrating that no one recognized it."

"What did Mr. Superstar do for a living?"

"He was a tax attorney. He needed a lot of attention. But he also needed a lot of reassurance and praise. It was as if he thought he was great, but he needed someone to confirm it all the time. *All* the time."

"That sounds exhausting."

"Mmm," Kit agreed, but only marginally. "It's just that there are a lot worse things than somebody who wants his partner in life to agree that he's the best thing since sliced bread. Both Bert and Tim were nice enough guys. They were kind and thoughtful. They remembered birthdays and anniversaries. They were loyal—neither of them ever cheated. They wanted to settle down, have families. In fact, they both had so many selling points that friends of mine snatched them up the minute I was out of the picture."

"They did?"

"They did. Bert got married last month to a sous-chef I went to school with and she considers herself lucky to have him. She says that after some of the men she dated or had serious relationships with, folding towels just right and alphabetizing canned goods in order to have the life she has with him is a very small price to pay. And the friend who's been seeing Tim since just after that un-wedding says she thinks he's as great as he thinks he is and she doesn't mind telling him so. She sees it as just being his support system and says that he's as supportive of her as he wants her to be of him."

"So you've just been left thinking it was all you," Ad surmised quietly, kindly.

"Well, it *was* all me. Tim and Bert were both right there, ready to walk down the aisle, willing to make the commitment, but I freaked out over nitpicky little things. It's just that I couldn't see myself spending the rest of my life folding towels to fit the exact size Bert had drawn for me on a piece of cardboard, or telling Tim every day that he really was the smartest, best, most undervalued person who ever lived."

"Seems reasonable to me."

"That I should fold towels according to specifications or bolster a man's ego every day?"

"No, that you should *not* want to do either of those things," Ad said. "I don't think they're nitpicky at all. Personally, I'd go crazy in either of those situations. It seems to me that you were wise to recognize that you didn't want to and that you got out before the weddings."

"*Barely* before the weddings," Kit corrected under her breath. Then, more to Ad, she said, "Most people think I just have commitment problems and when it comes right down to the actual moment of truth, I panic and run."

"What do you think?"

It was a question Kit had asked herself a hundred times. "I don't know," she said, giving him the only answer she'd ever come up with. "What I *do* know is that what kept going through my mind both times was the whole till-death-do-you-part thing. The rest of my life. Forever and ever—that's when I knew I couldn't walk down the aisle for either guy. I knew I couldn't promise that. I just couldn't. Even though it meant hurting them and embarrassing us both, embarrassing our families, wasting a ton of money and having to answer to everyone, I just couldn't do it. And believe me, the second time—knowing what it had been like to call off the first wedding—I didn't want to go through it all again. That's why I got to fifteen minutes before the ceremony—I was trying so hard not to bail *again*. But in the end…"

"Out the bathroom window," Ad supplied for her.

"Which was even worse for my family, for Tim, for his family. Everyone was there, in the church, dressed up and waiting for the no-show bride…"

Every ounce of how miserable Kit had felt over being the cause of all that echoed in her voice and sobered the mood.

"I know there are worse things people have done," she added quietly then. "But still, I caused a lot of pain and humiliation. And I did it *twice*."

"Okay, so maybe after doing it once you should have taken more things into consideration before you agreed to marry the second guy," Ad conceded. "But I'm still sticking with it being better to have recognized that you didn't want to spend the rest of your life with either of those guys and put an end to the relationships before you did marry them. Or have kids with them. As far as I can see, what you did—*twice*—was pretty damn brave. I know a lot of people who wouldn't have the courage to do it. I know one guy who *didn't* have the courage to do it even though he was having serious doubts at the last minute. He went through with the wedding, ended up unhappy and divorced within six months. Believe me, you'd be this guy's hero."

That made Kit laugh again, albeit a bit weakly. "Well, introduce me to that guy because, with the exception of Kira—who, as my best friend, has no choice but to tell me I'm okay—everyone else, including my family, just thinks I'm crazy."

Ad's oh-so-handsome face eased into a smile. "I think a lot of things about you but I don't think you're crazy."

She believed him. And oddly enough it made her feel better. It certainly helped her feel better about confiding all this in him.

He came out from behind the bar then and began to blow out the candles.

Kit turned to watch as he moved from one grouping to the next, enjoying the sight of his tall, lean body and the way his clothes accentuated every honed muscle.

She enjoyed the sight of him so much that she felt that same warmth erupting in her that he had elicited with the secret clasp of his hand when they'd said goodnight to Kira and Cutty.

But Kit fought it and said, "So if you think I'm brave and made the right choices in not marrying Tim or Bert, does that mean you aren't going to kick me out of the apartment in the name of your fellow men?"

"On behalf of Tidy-boy and Mr. Superstar?"

"Tidy-boy?" Kit repeated with another laugh.

"Neat-freak? Compulsive-man? Pick one."

"You are bad," Kit chastised, but not too seriously. She kept her eyes on Ad as he headed in her direction, extinguishing the candles as he did, until the place was lit by only a few candles still burning on the bar.

As he finished his task his gaze settled on her and something in his eyes let her know that telling him about her past definitely hadn't put him off.

Then he said, "No, I am not kicking you out on behalf of the guys you were smart enough not to marry. Why would I punish myself like that?"

"That would be punishment for you?"

She shouldn't have said that so flirtatiously. But that warmth inside her was gaining ground.

"I'd be losing out for sure," he said with a sexy half-smile and aquamarine eyes that delved into hers.

Kit leaned back against the bar, trapping her hands behind her. Those feelings Ad had inspired were making her itch to reach for him, and she hoped that pinning her hands would help keep her from doing it.

It didn't, however, keep Ad from coming toward her. Purposefully. Intently. His eyes still locked onto hers.

He came to stand directly in front of her and leaned just far enough forward to bracket her on either side with his arms and brace his weight on his hands where they clamped onto the edge of the bar.

"No, I am definitely not interested in kicking you out of the apartment for any reason," he reiterated in a voice that was low and husky and full of insinuation.

Clearly he wasn't horrified by her history the way she'd expected him to be. In fact, it just didn't seem to matter to him. At least not as much as whatever it was he had on his mind at that moment.

And whatever he had on his mind at that moment seemed to be igniting the air all around them with a charged sexual energy that was setting Kit aflame and warning her of what was to come.

She could have escaped before it did. She could have ducked under one of his arms and put distance between them to prove that she was opposed to whatever it was he had in mind. To demonstrate that she wasn't willing to let happen what had happened between them the last few nights—if that was where this was headed. And she was reasonably sure it was.

But she didn't budge. She didn't even tell him that she didn't want what had happened between them the last few nights not to happen again.

Because she did.

She didn't want to want it to happen again. She just couldn't help it.

So when Ad pushed a stray curl away from her temple and then laid his hand along the side of her face, she just let her eyelids drift partly downward, her chin tip partly upward. And she didn't offer any resistance at all when that hand at her cheek guided her head to a slight tilt that accommodated his mouth meeting hers.

There was something so perfect in that kiss. In the way their mouths melded. Perfect enough to instantly light a fire to those warm feelings that had been stirring inside her. And Kit was lost again, even more seriously than she had been when he'd kissed her the previous night. Lost in that man and how much she wanted to do exactly what they were doing.

His face moved against hers, brushing her nose with his slightly rough cheek, brushing her cheek with his chin, as his lips parted and brought hers along.

He let that hand at her face slide down to one shoulder, bringing his other hand to the opposite arm so both hands could follow the line of her arms and rescue them from their imprisonment behind her.

Once he had, he pulled them around him until her hands were flat against his back and then he retraced that path along her arms to wrap his around her as that kiss became deeper, more involved, mouths open wide and hungry, tongues teaching each other new tricks.

Kit raised a hand to his nape, wanting to feel more than his shirt even if it did encase his muscular back, wanting the feel of flesh. The feel of *his* flesh. Craving it beneath her hands, against her own skin.

But that wasn't the only craving she had.

Her breasts were alive with a craving of their own. With the nearly screaming need to have his hands on them. Or at the very least to be pressed to his chest. His bare chest.

As if that need had somehow been conveyed to him, Ad found the base of her spine with both hands then, slipping them underneath the hem of her square-cut top to her naked back.

Kit couldn't help writhing. Just a little. Into those big, strong hands. It just felt so good.

But as good as it felt, it felt even better when he began the slow caress that inched his hands higher and higher, increasing her anticipation, her desire to have them on her breasts, until he finally did what she'd yearned for him to do all along—he brought one hand around to discover an engorged globe.

The spaghetti straps of her top hadn't allowed for a bra and Kit had never been so glad of anything before. Because there it was—that agile, adept, talented hand covering her breast, letting her nipple harden in his palm.

A part-sigh, part-moan escaped her throat and her mouth opened wider still.

His hand kneaded her breast. Caressed it. Brushed feathery strokes all around it. And if that wasn't enough, he took her nipple between his thumb and index finger and tenderly rolled it into a knot so tight that it ached for even more.

Maybe so did Ad because a low moan rumbled in his chest and he deserted her breast suddenly to place both hands at the sides of her waist and lift her onto the bar as his mouth became even more demanding of hers, his tongue more insistent.

He found the hem of her skirt and pushed it up so he could finesse himself between her thighs, so her knees could ride his rib cage as his hands wasted no time gliding beneath her top again and reclaiming her breasts—both of them now—to drive her to a near frenzy.

But just as she was working up the courage to pull his shirt from his waistband and wondering how she could get him up on the bar with her, wondering what it would be like to make love there with him, her brain took a new turn. Without warning. All by itself.

A turn that shot her back to their conversation. To thoughts of those two weddings she'd run from. Those two men she'd left in the lurch. Those two times when she'd caused hurt and havoc.

And in spite of the fact that Ad had made her feel temporarily better about it all—or maybe *because* he had and she knew just what a good guy he was—she suddenly didn't think she could let this go any farther. Or let either of them get in any deeper than they already were.

So rather than pulling Ad's shirt free of his slacks,

she slid her hands around from his back to his chest—his massive, hard, phenomenal chest—and pushed herself away from him.

"I'm dangerous, remember?" she said breathlessly, even as she suffered instant second thoughts and couldn't help reveling in the feel of his chest beneath her palms.

"I like to live dangerously," he countered, kissing her neck, her shoulder, her collarbone, and then finding a very sensitive spot just below the hollow of her throat that she hadn't even known was sensitive before.

But she tried to ignore how much she wanted him to go on exploring that spot, consciously reminding herself of those other two men now so that she didn't lose sight of the need to end this before either she or Ad risked more than they already had.

"No, really," she said, dropping her brow to the top of Ad's head with a sort of finality and pushing against him slightly instead of fondling him.

That must have helped it register that she was serious.

Reluctantly he dropped his hands to her hips, only lightly resting them there as he stopped kissing her, pulled out from under her lowered head and met her eyes with his.

"And just when I was wondering how many restaurant health codes I'd be breaking if we used this bar for something other than serving drinks," Ad said then.

So they'd been on the same train of thought…

That made it even more difficult to refrain.

But still, Kit held tight to her decision. "I can't be responsible for bringing ruin down upon you," she joked in keeping with his health-code violations remark. But it applied in other respects, too, and she willed herself not to lose sight of that even though what she really—*really*—wanted was to have him up on the bar with her. Lying naked together there and most definitely using it for more than drinks…

Even without being given a genuine reason for why she'd stopped what had been happening between them, Ad conceded. He stepped back, put his hands on either side of her waist, and lifted her down to stand where she'd been before.

But he didn't concede completely because once she was there he left his hands on her sides and stared deeply into her eyes—maybe waiting for her to explain.

But when she didn't—and how could she when she just didn't know what to tell him—he took a deep breath, sighed it out elaborately, and said, "Oh, what you do to me."

Oh, what he did to her!

But Kit couldn't think about that right then. Not if she wanted to get out of there, away from him and all the temptations he presented.

"Big day tomorrow," she said as if that were reason enough to have ended something so good.

"That's what I understand," Ad answered, sounding distracted as he went on staring at her, searching her face, her eyes, with a heated gaze that made her wonder if he was going to kiss her again and restart everything. Making her wonder if her will would be strong enough to stop him a second time.

But luckily he didn't test her. After a moment he let go of her waist and instead took only one of her hands in his, bringing her with him to blow out the remainder of the candles.

Neither of them said anything as he led her through the swinging doors to the kitchen, out the alley door and up the stairs. And still Kit wasn't sure if that was where they were going to part or if what her body was crying out for was going to be satisfied after all.

But once more Ad didn't push it.

When they reached the landing he merely turned to face her, pulling the hand he held up between them and drawing patterns on the back of it with his thumb.

"I guess this is another good-night then," he said in that husky tone that remained in his voice.

"I guess it is," Kit agreed.

"So, good night."

"Good night."

But neither of them moved as Ad continued to rub her hand and they both watched him do it.

Then he raised that hand to his mouth and pressed a kiss where his thumb had been. A long, lingering kiss that just made her die to have it on her lips, instead.

But she held her breath and her ground, and after a moment he raised his eyes to hers once more and released her hand altogether.

And Kit knew she had to make her getaway or she'd be lost to her own screaming desires to finish what they'd started downstairs.

"Good night," she repeated, moving to her door

and making quick work of unlocking it and stepping inside.

But when she did she turned to look at Ad again, finding him watching her as intently as he had been when she'd been standing before him.

And he didn't answer her second good-night with another of his own. Instead he said, "You know, if I were Tidy-boy or Mr. Superstar, I don't think I would have given you up without a fight."

Kit couldn't help smiling a small smile at that before she said good-night a third time and closed her door.

Only to drop her head to the other side of it once she had, again fighting the raging desires he'd roused in her and thinking about what he'd just said.

Thinking that, while he might not have given her up without a fight if he'd been a part of her past, it was a good thing that he'd given up without a fight tonight.

Because if he hadn't, Kit knew that they would be on that bar downstairs right then…naked bodies and limbs entwined, violating every restaurant health code there was.

Chapter Eight

"Half an hour and it's all over for you, man," Ad warned Cutty as if his friend were about to walk to the gallows.

They were in the church basement at six-thirty on Saturday evening. Ad, Cutty and the other groomsmen had used the dressing room they'd been led to to get ready for the wedding, which was to begin at seven. Then the groomsmen had gone upstairs to usher guests to their seats, and Ad and Cutty had left the dressing room to wait in a common room where church meetings were held.

"Nervous?" Ad asked, more to goad Cutty than anything since Cutty was sitting in a folding chair with his feet up on a second one, looking perfectly at ease.

"Nope," the groom answered just as easily.

"Maybe you should think it over," Ad advised, turning a third folding chair so that the back was facing his friend and then straddling the seat. "This is it, you know? If you don't want to go through with tying yourself down to one woman for the rest of your life, now's the time to say it."

Cutty laughed. "Why wouldn't I want to go through with it? Kira is the smartest, sweetest, most beautiful, most wonderful woman in the world and she's not only willing to take on me and my kids, she's also uprooted her whole life to do it and done it without complaint. I'd need my head examined if I *didn't* tie myself down to her for the rest of my life. We just have to hope she doesn't change her mind."

"The way Kit did. Twice, apparently," Ad remarked, letting his friend in on the fact that he finally understood Cutty's remark about Kit's wedding track record.

But Cutty only grimaced at the information. "I'm not supposed to talk about that. I've been in trouble for shooting off my mouth about it and Kira made me promise I wouldn't do it again."

"It's okay. Kit told me everything."

"About both guys and not going through with either wedding?"

"About both guys and not going through with either wedding. And why."

"Kira says Kit was right to duck out both times—in case you care," Cutty said.

Ad *did* care. Even though there didn't seem to be a reason it should matter to him one way or another.

"From what Kit said about her fiancés," he said, "I thought she was right to duck out on them, too."

"Not that you wouldn't have to worry if you were in line to be number three," Cutty said.

"I guess you'd probably sweat it out right up to the *I do's,*" Ad agreed.

"I know I would."

For some reason that seemed to sober the tone slightly and from there a concern Ad had had about his friend popped up again, prompting him to address it.

"So, all kidding aside," he said. "Are you having any...I don't know—bad feelings about getting married again?"

Cutty shrugged. "I'm not having bad feelings about getting married, no. I'm off-the-chart happy to be doing this. But feelings that good raise some not-so-good things, yeah."

"Like what?"

Another shrug. "I don't know. It's just that a lot of times when I'm doing something that I really like doing or that's a sign that I'm going on with my life, I kind of have a twinge of guilt. I mean, Marla and Anthony aren't here, enjoying things, being off-the-chart happy, and I am. I guess that's where it comes from."

"And today there's that?"

"A little. But I try not to dwell on it when it happens. I have to think that their deaths were a part of some design that's grander than I'll ever be able to figure out, and that my being left to go on was a piece of it. And I think that making the best of that is what I'm supposed to do. The twins deserve it."

"You deserve it, too."

Cutty smiled. "I must, because it's like Kira was sent to me as a gift, and I can't help being grateful for that. As far as I'm concerned, after some rough patches in life, she was the one lucky thing that happened to me."

"True," Ad agreed.

"And you're jealous," Cutty added, turning the tables on him when it came to goading, and lightening the tone at the same time.

Ad laughed. And because it was Cutty, and Cutty had just confided in him, he reciprocated. "You're right. I am jealous."

"I knew it," Cutty gloated. "You'd like to be where I am."

And why, Ad wondered, did the image of Kit pop into his mind at that exact moment?

"It's no secret that I want to find somebody," Ad said. "It feels like my life won't really be started until that happens."

"It won't," Cutty confirmed.

"It's like I'm missing a spark plug and when I finally find it my engine will fire up and run."

"I don't know, you're engine seemed to be fired up and running pretty well this last week," Cutty pointed out.

Ad laughed again. "Yeah? How do you know?" he challenged.

"Your engine isn't just running, pal, it's racing so loud I can hear it."

"I think those are called auditory hallucinations," Ad countered rather than letting Cutty know he was right.

But Cutty persisted anyway. "Kit's great. I like her. Maybe you could break the pattern. The third time could be the charm, you know? Maybe you'd be the one she *doesn't* leave at the altar."

"And maybe you're just looking for somebody to keep you company now that you're about to take the leap."

"You know what they say—come on in, the water's fine."

Ad laughed yet again but all he said was, "Maybe we ought to concentrate on getting you married first and then we can work on me."

"Hey, I'm already there. It's your turn now."

Ad stood and pulled the chair Cutty was using for his feet out from under them. "I think I'll save my turn for later. Come on, let's go upstairs and see what kind of crowd you drew for this thing."

Kit hadn't wanted to eavesdrop on the exchange between Ad and Cutty in the church basement. But the room she needed to use to change clothes shared a wall with the room they were in and there was an uncloseable grate high up on that common wall.

The only way she could have avoided hearing what they'd said was if she had left the room. But since she'd done more to help Kira get ready than to get ready herself, she was down to the wire.

So while Kira was with the photographer sitting for her wedding portrait and the other bridesmaids were with her to watch, Kit had been left to hurry through her own dressing. Which had forced her to listen to what Ad and Cutty were talking about. Right up to the point where they'd left the other room.

Not that anything that had been said was so private she shouldn't have heard it. There hadn't been any deep, dark secrets revealed. It had been a simple chat between a couple of friends. Part of it about her...

It was that part of it that was still on her mind as she slipped on the flower-embroidered chemise dress.

Clearly both Ad and Cutty recognized that she was a bad risk when it came to marriage. But it didn't hurt her feelings. They were right—she was a bad risk. No one knew it better than Kit. No one was sorrier for it than Kit.

But actually, for some reason, it struck her as good that Ad was fully aware of it. Good that he didn't have any illusions about her. That his eyes were wide open.

In a way, it was freeing. It let her know that he didn't have expectations of her that she couldn't meet. It let her know that what was happening between them—the attraction, the kissing, the more-than-kissing of the night before—was closer to being a simple fling than anything serious, anything that could lead to the kind of far-reaching consequences and repercussions that had come out of her last two relationships.

Should it bother her that what was happening with Ad was only a fling? she asked herself as she took her hair out of the scrunchee that held it at her crown and bent far over to brush the unruly curls so they could be worn loose.

Maybe it should have bothered her. But it didn't.

Again, it just felt as if a burden had been lifted off her shoulders.

She was having a good time with Ad and she liked knowing that, in the process, she wasn't running any risk of disappointing him. Or hurting him. She liked knowing that there were no strings attached. That there was nothing to worry about.

In fact, it occurred to her the more she thought about it, that she hadn't felt that way since climbing out the window fifteen minutes before that last wedding. In the past seven months, every time she'd so much as considered dating again, she'd felt as if it would be unfair to even have dinner with someone or go to a movie with a man who didn't have any idea that he was out with someone who had left not one, but *two,* men at the altar. Two men who, just when they'd thought they could trust her the most, had had the rug pulled out from under them.

But Ad knew the worst about her. He had no illusions. And to Kit, that made him safe from the kind of pain and humiliation she'd inflicted on Bert and Tim. It relieved her of the nagging—if irrational—sense that she was a danger to him in some way.

She stood up straight once more, flinging her hair back as she did so it would fall away from her face.

And suddenly she realized that the coming evening—the wedding, being all dressed up, dining and dancing and drinking champagne—had a whole new appeal for her. A lighter feel to it.

She was going to have a wonderful time. With Ad. And without any qualms or trepidations. She was going to enjoy Ad's company without worrying about a single thing.

She took a look at herself in the full-length mirror she was standing in front of, judging the final product as she let herself relax more completely than she thought she had in seven months.

The dress fit the way she remembered, barely brushing the lines of her figure from the spaghetti straps down to her ankles. She squared her shoulders to more fully fill out the built-in bra hidden behind the slight drape of fabric at the bustline, and all in all, she judged herself presentable enough not to feel self-conscious about the way she looked.

It was definitely going to be a good night, she decided, slipping her feet into the strappy shoes that had been dyed to match the dress and then applying the pale lipstick she and Kira had picked out earlier in the week as the final touch of makeup added to the blush, mascara and eyeliner she'd put on earlier.

"Kit? We need you for pictures," someone called through the door.

"I'll be right there," she called in return, craning around to make sure she looked okay from the back, too.

Then she took a final glimpse of the whole picture, pushed her breasts up a bit higher so that a hint of cleavage showed above the straight-across neckline, and headed for the door.

With no doubts whatsoever that it was going to be an absolutely perfect night for Kira.

And a pretty terrific one for Kira's best friend, too.

* * *

The wedding ceremony itself lasted about half an hour and through it all Kit had trouble not sneaking peeks at Ad. As the best man and maid of honor, they stood on either side of Cutty and Kira, facing them to be witness to the event. And facing each other as a result.

It might have helped if Ad hadn't looked so strikingly handsome dressed in his black tuxedo, a crisp white shirt and bow tie. But as it was, the tux couldn't have been tailored more impeccably and it only accentuated the breadth of his shoulders, the expanse of his chest, the narrowness of his waist and hips, the length and strength of his legs. And all with a suaveness and sophistication that was nearly devastating to behold.

It also didn't help that his hair was artfully disarrayed, his face was freshly shaven, and he stood with his hands clasped low in front of him—large, powerful-looking hands that Kit kept remembering the feel of on her bare breasts.

So it was no surprise that she struggled to keep her mind on the heartfelt vows being spoken nearby. A struggle made more difficult by the fact that Ad's aquamarine eyes strayed to her every few minutes, too. Eyes that seemed to burn with intensity—or maybe with the same memories of the previous evening…

Kira and Cutty were pronounced man and wife in the midst of Kit's preoccupation and met by a round of applause that she knew would make her friend feel all the more accepted. Then there were additional photographs taken and everyone went on to the reception that was being held in the town square.

A huge white tent had been erected for the occasion and beside it was a wooden platform that served as a dance floor and stage for the band. Under the tent were strands and strands of tiny white lights strung along the inside, while hundreds more formed a bright canopy over the dance platform outside.

The tent protected round tables covered in linen tablecloths, each with a spray of white roses and candles to add more illumination for diners who feasted on crab puffs, smoked salmon, and stuffed artichoke heart appetizers; salads of fresh arugula, spinach and baby endive dressed in French vinaigrette; beef Wellington or roasted game hens for the main course, accompanied by grilled baby vegetables and sweet potato puree laced with brandy and pecans.

Kit's cake was the centerpiece, and not only was the towering confection so beautiful it brought tears to Kira's eyes when she told Kit so, it was the talk of the wedding reception even before it had been cut.

Once it was, Kit was glad she had made more layers than she ordinarily would have for the number of invited guests because so many people went back for seconds and even thirds.

Then the music began, and Kira and Cutty had their first dance as man and wife while everyone looked on.

It was watching that dance that brought tears to Kit's eyes. She knew Kira as well as she knew her own sisters, and she could see how happy her best friend was, how complete Cutty made her feel.

But Kit managed to contain the tears until Kira and Cutty paused in their dance to each pick up one of the twins—adorable in their ruffly white dresses—and return to dance as a family. That was when even madly blinking her eyes wasn't enough to contain Kit's emotions.

"Need this?"

It was Ad's voice coming from beside her as he leaned sideways to ask that question so no one else would hear, subtly holding out his handkerchief to her.

Kit laughed a little soggily, accepting it to dab at the moisture that rolled down her cheeks.

But she was afraid her mascara had run and so, without looking Ad in the eye, she did a minor wave of the handkerchief and said, "I just...I'll bring this back," and turned to make her way through the guests.

Directly across the street to the east of the town square, the ice cream parlor had closed for business so the owners could attend the wedding. But the front door was unlocked in order for guests to use their rest rooms. That was where Kit went.

It didn't seem like something as small as a trip to the bathroom—where Kit found her smudge-proof mascara was trustworthy—could have changed the course of the rest of the evening. But somehow it did. Before that Ad had been by her side—through the picture taking, through dinner, through the cutting and serving of the cake.

But when Kit returned to the celebration it became impossible to reconnect with him.

Not that she didn't try. Or that he didn't. It was just that every time they made it to within a few feet of each other something prevented them from getting any closer.

There were just so many people who wanted to meet Kit or talk to her about the cake or about hiring her to make one for them or someone they knew. There were so many friends of Ad's who wanted to talk to him or slap him on the back, so many who apparently hadn't seen him recently and wanted to ask if he was fully recovered from the head injury he'd incurred saving the family from the burning house earlier in the summer.

And before Kit knew it, the evening was waning, guests were beginning to leave, and there were even more people who didn't want to go without thanking her for that cake and telling her how nice it had been to meet her.

Until, by midnight when Kira and Cutty left amidst a hail of well-wishes and catcalls, all Kit could think was that she hadn't had a single moment alone with Ad. And that maybe she'd been wrong when she'd thought she was in for a pretty terrific night tonight.

Although about the time she thought that, she felt someone step up behind her. Close enough to whisper in her ear.

"I say that if the bride and groom can take off, so can the maid of honor and the best man. What do you say?"

Kit didn't have to see him to know it was Ad.

"I say I agree," she answered, staring straight ahead and trying not to smile too big.

Ad stepped to her side, motioning with one index finger to a path that led out of the tent. "Then let's go before somebody else wants to talk to you about that damn cake and I get shoved out of the way for them to do it."

"*Damn* cake? I beg your pardon," Kit said, pretending to be offended when she knew exactly what he was talking about.

"Wonderful damn cake, but damn cake just the same," he insisted. "I thought I was going to get to dance every dance with you and instead I haven't even seen you. Thanks to that damn cake and the bump on my head."

"That *damn* bump on your head," Kit amended.

"That damn bump on my head," he agreed as they finally left the tent—amazingly, without being delayed by anyone.

Beyond the tent and the lights and candles, the surrounding town square was quiet and much darker in spite of the tall ornate wrought-iron pole lamps that illuminated it. But to Kit the change was welcome.

"Now our only problem," Ad said once they were there, "is that I'm car-less. I could probably snag us a ride but we're only a few blocks from home, so how about if we walk it?"

Even though Kit's strappy high-heeled shoes were killing her feet, the idea of walking alone with Ad was still preferable to having to share him with anyone with transportation.

"Hang on," she advised, bending to slip off her shoes.

Ad was quick to take her elbow to steady her and Kit tried not to notice the tiny embers that seemed to ignite in her at even that brief, innocent contact.

But even so, she missed it when she'd finished removing her shoes and he let go.

"Great idea," he said then. "I think I'm going to do a little of that myself."

But it wasn't shoes he took off. He shrugged out of his jacket, untied his bow tie to stuff in the jacket pocket, and unfastened his collar button and the two below it.

It must have felt good because he rolled his head around, stretching his thick neck and sighing like a contented cat as he did.

"Better?" Kit asked, savoring the sight.

"Much," he assured.

Then he hooked the coat on two fingers and slung it over his shoulder before they really did begin to walk in the direction of the restaurant.

"Thanks for the use of your handkerchief, by the way," Kit said into the pleasant silence of the night as they strolled at a leisurely pace. "I tried to say that when I gave it back to you but someone interrupted me."

"Anytime."

"I don't usually cry at weddings," she said. Then she laughed wryly and added, "I usually run from them."

Ad chuckled at that. "I didn't want to be the one to say it," he joked.

"I was just happy for Kira. And Cutty."

"I'm happy for them, too," Ad said, making Kit recall what she'd overheard him say about not feeling as if his life had really begun until he found someone to marry.

But she also reminded herself that he wasn't counting on her to be that person, that they were merely having a pleasant—short-lived—interlude, and that there was no pressure on her for anything else. And she relaxed all over again the way she had in that dressing room earlier.

"I still can't believe they were allowed to take up the whole town square for the reception, though," Kit commented.

"It's a small town, remember? A close community. The town square is sort of like a communal backyard. Anybody can use it. But if you do, it makes it hard to keep the guest list down."

"And it seemed like everyone who was invited showed up," Kit remarked.

"It's also hard to *not* go to anything you're invited to in a town this size. You can't lie to get yourself out of it because everybody knows what everybody else is doing most of the time," Ad explained wryly.

"The whole thing is kind of amazing, though. I mean, it was one couple's wedding but it was treated almost like a holiday. Businesses closed, even the local radio station dedicated the whole day's music to Kira and Cutty, and only played love songs. I've never seen anything like it."

"I would have thought you'd done the cakes for enough weddings to see everything."

"I have seen a lot," Kit conceded.

"Tell me the weirdest," Ad requested as they stepped onto the sidewalk at the south end of a deserted Main Street.

"The weirdest…" Kit repeated, trying to decide. "I

think there's more than one that qualifies. But one of the weirdest was the wedding in the nudist camp."

That made Ad laugh. "Did you have to deliver the cake in the buff?"

He sounded intrigued by the possibility.

"It was optional. I opted to wear clothes. So did some of the guests. But none of the wedding party did."

"So no tuxedos there," Ad said with a chuckle.

"No. Just bouquets for the women and bow ties for the men."

"Around the guys' necks, I hope."

It was Kit's turn to laugh again. "Yes, around the guys' necks," she said, chastising him for his insinuation.

"What about underwater weddings or parachuting weddings?" he asked then. "Have you done any of those?"

"I actually did do one where the ceremony was performed on a plane, in the air, and the couple parachuted into the reception afterward. Unfortunately the wind shifted in the middle of the jump and instead of landing on the dance floor the way they'd planned, the bride hit the buffet table and the groom landed in my cake."

"Ohhh, that's bad," Ad said as they reached the restaurant.

He unlocked the door and they went in. But they didn't bother to turn on any lights as they passed through the dining room and kitchen to go out the rear door into the alley.

"I also did a vampire wedding," Kit told him along the way.

"Vampire?"

"Well, vampire aficionados."

"Let me guess—it was a Halloween wedding?"

"Bingo. Everyone was dressed like something out of a gothic nightmare, complete with glue-on fangs. Although one woman was so into it that she'd had her dentist make permanent fangs for her," Kit said as they climbed the steps. "The cake had to be decorated with black frosting and instead of flowers or anything pretty, they wanted it to look like each layer was dripping blood."

"Yuk," Ad said. "That's worse than the nudist colony."

They reached the landing and Kit was sorry it had been such a short walk. After having looked forward to spending the entire evening with Ad—her next-to-last evening in Northbridge—just the past few minutes with him hadn't been nearly enough.

But he didn't seem in any hurry to end their time together himself because he draped his tuxedo jacket over the landing's corner post and leaned back against the railing, stretching out first one leg and then the other in a wide V that braced his weight on the heels of his feet.

"You know, this wasn't how tonight was supposed to go," he informed her then.

Unsure what he was referring to, Kit said, "I thought the wedding came off without a hitch."

"It did. I wasn't talking about the wedding."

Was she mistaken or had his voice lowered an octave? To a seductive, sensuous timbre…

"What were you talking about? The dancing again?" Kit asked, remembering his comment that he'd intended to dance every dance with her tonight.

"Partly the dancing. But mostly I'd just thought I'd get to be with you all night."

All night?

"And what did you have in mind if dancing was only part of it?" she heard herself ask in a tone that had come out surprisingly suggestive itself.

Ad leaned forward far enough to bracket her waist with his hands and pull her toward him until she was standing in the V of his out-stretched legs. "I thought maybe I'd get the chance to convince you that you aren't as dangerous as you think you are."

As dangerous as she'd told him she was the previous night when she'd stopped what had been happening between them.

"I know two men who would disagree with you," she said. But she said it with a flirtatious lilt to her voice because now that she knew his eyes were open when it came to her, she didn't feel as if she was putting him in any kind of jeopardy.

Ad smiled at her, a calm, confident smile. "I know someone who might tell *you* to run like hell away from a hick like me."

Hick? Maybe his former fiancée hadn't seen him dressed in a tuxedo...

Ad clasped his hands together at the small of her back, bringing her even closer so he could kiss her. Just once. Barely.

Then he said, "Do you want to run like hell from me?"

"No," she confessed, raising her hands to his chest even as she considered what she might be getting herself into.

But tonight was different. Tonight she had that new sense of freedom keeping her as calm as he seemed to be. Tonight she was willing to just let what had been simmering since she'd met this man take its course because she knew he wasn't thinking too far in the future and so it didn't seem like she had to, either.

"Okay," Ad said. "If I'm not afraid of you and you don't want to run from me…" He kissed her again, lingering slightly this time before he stopped to continue what he was saying. "Maybe we can salvage tonight after all."

"Maybe we can," Kit said as she tilted her head to accommodate his third kiss.

And despite the fact that she was fully aware of every nuance of it, of every detail of having his mouth on hers, of his lips doing a lazy reacquaintance with hers, she still offered herself the chance not to let it go any farther than they had in the past.

But the truth was, when she really, honestly thought about it, she realized that she wanted it to go farther. She'd been so attracted to this man, so enamored of him, so just plain hot for him, that she knew if she didn't let it go all the way she would spend the rest of her life wondering if it could have been as incredible with him as she suspected it could.

And she didn't want to be left wondering.

So she let her hands move up Ad's chest to his shoulders, then to the nape of his neck as she deepened the kiss, parting her lips a bit more than they'd been parted.

Ad answered in kind and one-upped her by sending his tongue to greet first the inner rim of her lips, then the tips of her teeth, and only then, her tongue, too.

But just when she thought she'd relayed the right signals—signals that she hoped encouraged him to go on—Ad ended that kiss, too, laying his brow to the top of her head.

"Tell me where to go from here," he ordered in a quiet, husky tone.

Apparently her signals hadn't been as clear as she'd thought.

"Where to go?" she repeated, wondering if it was merely a your-place-or-mine question.

But it wasn't because he said, "I don't want to end up like last night."

"Frustrated and confused?" Kit asked with a note of levity.

"Mmm. And wondering if I overstepped my bounds."

"You didn't," she was quick to assure.

"Then where do we go from here?" he reiterated.

Last chance to chicken out, she told herself. But she didn't need a last chance. She knew exactly where she wanted them to go from there. "How about inside?" she whispered.

"No kidding?"

"No kidding."

Kit sensed him smile.

Then he asked what she'd hoped he was asking before, "Inside my place or yours?"

"They're both yours," she reminded. "But since I've never been inside *your* yours and I have no idea if there are whips and chains and handcuffs waiting in there, let's use my side."

This time she got to see his smile because he straightened up so he could look into her eyes. "I don't even have glue-on fangs, let alone whips or chains or handcuffs. But the nudist thing? I'm all for that."

Kit smiled herself, thinking how comfortable she always felt with him. Even now. Even embarking on what they were about to embark on.

Comfortable enough to move out of the circle his arms formed around her and take his hand to lead him first to her door, then, once she'd unlocked it, inside the studio apartment.

But that was the end of her leading him. Once they were in the moonlit room Ad spun her around and pulled her close up against him, finding her mouth with his again in a kiss that was nothing like those that had preceded it, a kiss that was open-mouthed and hungry right from the start.

Kit answered with a hunger of her own. Now that she'd made her decision to do this, it was as if everything she'd been suppressing had been unleashed and she wanted him so desperately she had to put effort into not ripping his clothes off.

Still, she couldn't contain the urge enough to keep herself from unbuttoning his shirt and pulling the tails from his pants so she could plunge her hands into the open front and lay her bare palms to the warm satin of his honed pectorals.

Oh, but that was so much better than having his shirt separating them.

Only now, all she could think about was that it would be better still if her dress was off and his hands were on her, too.

Tonight he didn't read that thought as rapidly as he had the night before, though. Or, if he did, he was sticking to his own pace.

What he did do was cup both of her shoulders in those big hands of his and knead them in the identical way she wanted his hands on her breasts.

It was nice and it felt good, it was just that there were so many other portions of her body crying out for attention.

Maybe *that* was what he tuned into because after another moment at her shoulders he moved on to her collarbone and when he returned to her shoulders it was with the spaghetti straps of her dress in tow, taking them down to her arms.

Kit sighed into that increasingly passionate kiss to let him know that he was on the right track, and in reward he reached around to the back of her dress and unzipped it.

There wasn't much shape to the bridesmaid's gown and with the straps already off, once the zipper was open, it floated into a little heap around her ankles, leaving her clad only in thigh-high nylons and lacy thong bikini panties.

But Kit didn't feel shy or embarrassed the way she thought she might. She just felt like she wanted some company.

So she brought her own hands over his shoulders and eased his shirt off, letting it fall to the floor behind him.

Apparently Ad had no complaint with that. Actually he seemed to take it as a cue and before Kit had to do more, he kicked off his shoes and dropped the tuxedo pants, too.

Curiosity struck Kit then.

Was he wearing anything at all? Or was he completely naked? Right there, where she could look at him? Touch him?

That curiosity made her bold and she sent her hands exploring. From his broad back where her hands had ended up after she'd removed his shirt, down to his waist, forward to his hips and down a little farther, to his thighs... No, there weren't any shorts. There was only warm, smooth flesh over firm muscle.

He wrapped his arms around her then, kissing her continuously, but more playfully now, as he began to move them both toward the bed.

When they reached it he even managed to ease them down so they could lie side by side on the mattress without abandoning her mouth.

But once she was there he stopped kissing her to look first into her eyes, then let his gaze roll slowly down her body.

A groan of admiration followed that first look at her before he got up and began a studied removal of her nylons.

Kit didn't mind. Not only did she want to be rid of every shred of clothing the way he was, but it also gave her the opportunity to finally get to see him.

And he was definitely something to see!

Something so incredible she thought that it should never be covered. Tall and straight and broad-shouldered, his stomach was flat and rippled with muscle, his biceps and thighs could have been cut by a sculptor's knife, and that part of him that made him all man stood long and hard and proud.

When he'd rid her of nylons and panties he came back to lie beside her on the bed. To recapture her mouth with his, to brace his weight on one elbow and comb his fingers through her hair, to caress the side of her face with his other hand.

But there was even more intensity in it all now. Even more urgency and hunger and need, sending that caressing hand into motion. Gliding down her back, along her hip to her thigh, cupping her fanny to pull her snuggly against him, against that steely staff that proved he wanted her.

Kit held tight to him and did some caressing of her own down the narrowing V of his back to his waist, farther down to slightly dig her fingers into that honed derriere that had so often caught her eye.

But still her breasts screamed for attention and her spine arched in answer, pressing taut, demanding nipples into his chest.

This time Ad didn't hesitate. That searching hand of his coursed its way to her breast, taking it fully into his grip.

Kit couldn't keep from moving against him and together they were like a sailboat gliding smoothly, effortlessly along the waves, rolling with each swell as if they were being carried along by them.

Mouths clung together and then parted. Ad kissed her chin, her cheek, her jawbone, the sensitive lobe of her ear, the side of her neck.

Kit did some of that herself—kissing from his collarbone to his shoulder, then to the mound of muscled pectoral just above a tightened male nib of his own.

But when Ad began to follow a similar path, Kit gave way, letting her head fall backward, her shoulders straightening to allow him free access.

Wondrous lips and hot, flicking tongue trailed from the hollow of her throat down to the first rise of her breast, not hesitating to go lower, to trace her nipple with the pointed tip of that tongue before taking it into his mouth, engulfing her breast in that warm, wet wonder.

His free hand went lower still, reaching between her legs to that spot that was awakening with a yearning that was beginning to overwhelm her.

Gentle fingers introduced themselves, seeking, learning, driving her to a near frenzy.

But just when she thought she couldn't hold back one minute more, Ad seemed to know that he'd taken her to the brink. In a whisk of strong arms he turned her from her side to lie flat on the bed and moved over her, replacing his hand with his whole body now positioned between her thighs. Thighs that spread for him, that welcomed him joyfully and with so much anticipation that Kit could barely breathe.

He didn't disappoint her. He slipped into her with a slow, careful insistence until he filled her completely with the heat and strength of his body.

But just when she expected more, less was what she got. Less movement. A slowing of everything as Ad cupped both sides of her face in his hands and kissed her again, merely pulsing inside her while he did.

Never had another kiss seemed to touch something so deep and primal within her as that kiss did, leaving her even more desperately in need of relief.

Then he took most of his weight on his forearms and began to move once again, thrusting into her in a rhythmic unity that felt too divine for Kit to believe. Up and down, in and out, weightless and weighted at once, pressing her into the softness of the mattress until she answered by raising her hips to meet him, to pull him completely into her.

Faster and faster they moved together. Riding blissfully over wild and choppy seas, until she couldn't keep up and could only grasp the expanse of his magnificent back and let herself be carried to the heights of that journey. Carried into an all-engulfing, all-encompassing, blinding ecstasy that burst into a million points of light to steal her breath and all sense of time and space, to meld them together as he reached that same peak, to loosen any ties of gravity and soar for one mindless moment in pure, shared physical rapture.

And when it was over and they were both replete, he

again arched his upper body so he could cup her face in his hands, looking down at her as if he wanted to memorize every line, every detail of her face.

"That was like nothing I've ever known," he said in a raspy, awe-filled voice. "Are you okay?"

Kit smiled up at him, marveling at all that had just happened and at the warmth that washed through her just to be looking at his face.

"Very okay," she assured.

He kissed her once more and then left her to lie on his back, using one arm to scoop her over close beside him and clasping his other arm around her once she was.

It felt like the perfect place to be at that moment, their bodies forming to one another so that hard met soft, and hills met valleys, and Kit let her head be pillowed by his chest as her eyelids suddenly became so heavy she couldn't keep them open.

And all she could think as she was gently tugged toward sleep was that she'd been right after all.

This had been a pretty terrific night for Kira's best friend.

The most terrific night Kit had ever spent.

Chapter Nine

"Ad! Man, where are ya?"

That voice in the distance brought Ad out of the deep sleep he was in. When it did, it occurred to him that the door knocking he'd thought he'd been dreaming about must have been real.

"Ad! You gotta be in there. Wake up! We need the keys."

The voice belonged to his fry cook, and it was coming from outside. But not directly outside. Outside at the door to Ad's apartment. Because, of course, his fry cook had no way of knowing Ad was in the studio apartment instead. With Kit. In bed with Kit. In a bed he wanted to stay in, with Kit curled up beside him.

And now that he was awake, there were a lot of things he would rather do than open up the restaurant for Sunday breakfast.

But his fry cook wasn't going away and the rest of the kitchen staff was probably downstairs waiting to go to work, and, before too long, customers would be showing up.

Damn.

Ad took a deep breath, sighed and opened his eyes, knowing that no matter how much he wanted to stay right where he was, it wasn't fair to anybody—including Kit, who couldn't sleep through much more of the fry cook's attempts to rouse him. So, being careful not to jostle her, he slipped out of bed.

His tuxedo pants were on the floor where he'd left them and he paused to pull them on before he went to the door, opened it and stepped out onto the landing.

"Morning, Mike," he said quietly just as the fry cook was raising a fist to pound on the door again.

"There you are," the fry cook said, sounding relieved. But then he took in the sight of Ad shirtless and barefoot, in rumpled tuxedo pants, and relief turned to a knowing grin. "I didn't think to knock on the *other* door," the nineteen-year-old added then.

Ad ignored the innuendo, took his keys from his pants pocket, unlocked the door to his own apartment and, without opening it, handed the entire ring to his employee.

"Let everybody in and leave these under the bar. I'll get them back when I come down in a little while," he informed the still-grinning cook.

"Sure. No hurry. We all know what to do to get things going."

"Good," Ad answered.

"Big night last night, huh?" the fry cook said then.

"Go to work, Mike," Ad advised rather than answering that, giving the younger man a hard stare to warn him off any more questions.

Mike got the message. "Sure," he said, moving around Ad to go down the stairs to the alley door and use the keys he'd just been given.

Ad knew that within the next five minutes every member of his staff would know where he'd spent the previous night. But there was nothing he could do about it. And at that moment he was more interested in getting back to where he'd spent the previous night. So that's what he did, returning to the studio apartment as quietly as he'd left it.

But he discovered that not everything had remained the same when he moved silently to the side of the bed.

Kit had rolled to the center, taking up almost the entire space now, and she was sleeping so angelically that guilt washed through Ad for thinking of waking her. Even if he was itching for another round of what they'd done several times through the night.

Would she mind? he wondered.

Maybe not. But maybe she would. Especially since he hadn't let her get more than an hour or two of rest.

And he really should go to his place, he reasoned. He needed to shower, to shave. And he should at least check in at the restaurant.

Damn.

Although he did feel better about letting Kit sleep when he thought that maybe if she snoozed while he showered and shaved and checked in downstairs, then he could come up here and wake her in an hour without feeling as guilty.

He liked that idea.

So he silently gathered his clothes and once again left the studio apartment, this time fostering visions of how he wanted to spend the time until they were due at Kira and Cutty's at noon for the gift-opening brunch that would end the wedding events.

But as he dumped his things on the sofa in his living room and went through his bedroom into the bathroom there, that brunch and it being the last of the wedding events struck him.

With the end of the wedding that was the only reason Kit was in Northbridge, she would be going home. To Denver.

And she'd be going home to Denver soon.

Maybe even later today or tonight. Probably tomorrow at the latest since that was when Kira and Cutty were taking off on their honeymoon.

Ad had turned on the water in the shower but for a moment he didn't step under it. He just stood there while the fact that Kit would be leaving sank in.

Kit would be *leaving*.

It hit him like a ton of bricks.

He didn't want her to go.

That was a sentiment he was familiar with, he thought as he finally forced himself to move.

How many times had he felt that way when he was with Lynda?

Too many to count.

And here he was, feeling it all over again.

Stronger, even, than he'd felt it with Lynda.

How the hell had that happened? And so damn fast?

But he didn't have to think too hard to know how it had happened. Or why it hadn't taken much time.

He was crazy about Kit. He'd been crazy about her almost from the first minute he'd laid eyes on her. And if ever there was chemistry between two people it had been between him and Kit. He'd known it all along.

But he'd also known that she was an out-of-towner—the one big red flag on the play. And he'd figured that knowing that was enough to keep him from getting in too deep. That knowing it was the fail-safe feature.

Apparently that wasn't true.

Apparently he couldn't go blithely on his way, spending time with her, getting to know her, kissing her, making love to her, and expect that that knowledge—that she came with the same drawback Lynda had come with—was enough to keep him from falling for her.

Because he *had* fallen for her.

Brother, had he fallen for her.

Finished with his shower, Ad turned off the water and yanked his towel from the rack, drying himself with punishing strokes.

She lives in Denver, he reminded himself. *She has her business there. And you're here. It's Lynda all over again and you walked right into it.*

But the more he thought about it, the more he realized that, when it came to the logistics, it was true that he was in the same boat with Kit that he'd been in with Lynda. But maybe it wasn't so true that he was in the same boat in other respects. Important respects.

Like when it came to the actual relationship he had with Kit.

Ultimately, he and Lynda had been so different. They'd kept different hours. They'd been interested in different things. Their likes and dislikes when it came to food, to entertainment, to other people, had been different. They'd had different goals and ambitions and visions of the future. Certainly they'd had different opinions about what he should do for a living.

But none of that was true with Kit. With Kit everything had meshed. They'd connected on every level. There was just something that felt so right about them being together.

Of course that didn't change the logistical problems, which were the same logistical problems he'd had with Lynda, he thought as he stepped up to the sink to shave.

And the logistical problems were major problems.

But what if, by some stretch of the imagination, Kit moved to Northbridge?

Okay, maybe that was a tremendous stretch of the imagination. But still, what if she did? What about the fact that Lynda had never made friends or fit in here? The fact that she'd hated small town life? How did Kit compare in that regard?

Ad didn't have to think about that for long to come to the conclusion that Kit already fit in better than Lynda ever had. The night that Kit had waited tables for him there had been glaring evidence of how well she fit in. And she'd been so popular at the wedding that it had infringed on his plans to have her all to himself.

Then, too, Northbridge didn't seem to grate on Kit like it had on Lynda. Granted Kit had only been here a short time, but Lynda had griped about it from the start, and, with Kit, there hadn't been any complaining at all. In fact, she seemed to appreciate the small town. To enjoy the sense that everyone was one big family.

"But you can't seriously think she might chuck everything in Denver and move here just because you ask her to," he said to his reflection in the mirror.

Maybe he couldn't *seriously* think that. But he also couldn't deny that, deep down, there was a spark of hope that it wasn't completely out of the realm of possibility.

A spark of hope that set him to thinking about how terrific it would be to have her there with him on more than a temporary basis. To have her in his life. To have more nights like the last one.

To have a lifetime of nights like the last one.

A lifetime?

That might be a big leap when it came to Kit, he reminded himself, suddenly thinking of her history. After all, she'd basically left two guys at the altar. That was hardly something he should be forgetting.

And what about that? What about the fact that twice she'd made commitments she hadn't kept?

He'd told Cutty he thought she was right to do it and

even thinking about it now, he still believed that. It was just tough to ignore the fact that she had. Tough not to think about it in regards to himself.

What if he somehow managed to talk her into moving to Northbridge and set the wheels into motion for them to have a future together, and just about the time he thought that was going to come about, she bailed on him the way she had on those other two guys?

It wouldn't be good, that was for sure.

It would be damn *bad.*

And if he was worried about running that risk then maybe he should just forget the whole thing. Forget everything he was thinking and considering. Maybe he should just count himself lucky to have had this time with her and let her go back to Denver.

And never see her again.

Except that just the thought of that made him feel lousy. Lousier than he'd felt when things hadn't worked out with Lynda. Too lousy to ignore.

Lousy enough to let him know he couldn't just forget the whole thing.

Or her…no matter what she might have done in the past.

So where did that leave him?

"You're going to have to at least talk to her," he told his reflection as he wiped away residual shaving foam from his chin and cheeks.

And it was true, he *was* going to have to talk to her.

Because even though he knew he was running the risk of her laughing in his face now or of things not working out later on, if he didn't let her know how he felt and what he wanted, then there was no chance at all for anything beyond what they'd already had together.

And he wanted it to go beyond that.

He wanted it bad.

Bad enough that he had to at least give it a try.

Because the more he thought about it, the more he realized something.

He'd told Cutty that he felt like his life wouldn't actually begin until he'd found the woman he wanted to spend it with and he'd meant that. But what he realized now was that since he'd met Kit he'd felt as if that had happened.

And now that it had, he couldn't just let the person who had inspired it slip through his fingers.

He had to do whatever he could to hold on to her.

Kit was sound asleep when the smell of coffee lured her awake. Strong, hot coffee.

But she was *sooo* tired.

Coffee could wait.

She snuggled more firmly into her pillow.

"Come on, sleepyhead, wake up…"

That made her smile. It was Ad's voice. Nearby. Soft and coaxing and as tempting as the man himself.

And he was tempting. He'd tempted her all night long. And she'd succumbed. All night long…

Coffee might not be worth waking up for, but Ad was.

Her smile got bigger and she opened her eyes to mere slits.

He was sitting on the edge of the bed, facing her and holding a steaming cup right under her nose.

"No fair," she groaned.

But she opened her eyes the rest of the way, rolled to her back and—making sure she had a hold of the sheet to keep her naked body covered—she sat up.

Only then did she notice that Ad was showered, shaved and dressed in a pair of jeans and a sunny yellow polo shirt, and that he smelled like heaven.

"You've been awake for a while," she observed, accepting the coffee with one hand but still keeping the sheet over herself with the other.

"Awhile," he confirmed. "My staff needed to be let in to work and you were sleeping so sweetly I thought I'd let you stay that way for a little longer."

"And now you're all cleaned up and I'm a mess," she said, worrying about just how much of a mess she might be.

Ad smiled an appreciative smile. "You look adorable," he said as if he meant it. "If I didn't have something I need to talk to you about before I bust I'd be crawling in that bed with you now instead of bringing you coffee."

"You have to talk to me about something before you bust?" she reiterated, thinking that having him crawl into bed with her was more appealing than any conversation.

"I just needed to tell you how great this last week with you has been for me."

Hearing that sent little goose bumps up Kit's arms and made her smile all over again. "For me, too," she admitted.

"So, let's play *what if*," he suggested enthusiastically.

"What if? That's what you're busting to do?"

"Uh-huh."

"Okay…" Kit agreed without masking her confusion.

"Okay. For instance, what if Colorado passed a law that banned Kit's Cakes?"

Kit laughed. "Why would they do that? Because I put too much butter in the frosting? Because I use imported chocolate instead of domestic?"

"For whatever reason. No more Kit's Cakes in Colorado. You can do it anywhere else in the world, but not in Colorado. Would you consider moving to Montana to make wedding cakes?"

Oh. Maybe this wasn't a good game to be playing.

But now that it had begun, she supposed she had to go along with it.

So, tentatively, she said, "Montana in general, or did you have a specific location in mind?"

"Let's say Northbridge."

"Northbridge," Kit repeated uncertainly.

"Right."

"This is kind of a strange game," she said.

But Ad wasn't inclined to call it off. "If you had to move, would Northbridge be anywhere on the list of possible relocations?" he persisted. "Keeping in mind that your best friend in the world lives here."

And also keeping in mind that he did, too? Was that what he was getting at?

"I don't think Colorado is going to ban my cakes," she hedged.

"Hypothetically. Would you consider moving to Northbridge if they did?"

"It's a nice little town," she conceded carefully.

"So you haven't felt claustrophobic here or missed big city life or thought you might go out of your mind if you have to see the same faces one more time?"

All the things that his former fiancée had hated about the place.

"Well, no, none of that," Kit admitted but without oomph.

"Okay. Good. Now let's play what if the only guy left on the face of the earth owned and ran a restaurant and bar—would you spend the rest of your life alone rather than have to sink to the level of hanging out with him?"

More of what his former fiancée had found fault with.

This was making Kit increasingly uneasy. "You know that's not *sinking* to any level for me. I bake cakes for a living, that's on par with the restaurant and bar business. And I've done plenty of time as a waitress."

"Okay. Good. Now let's play what if I said I realized this morning that I can't stand the thought of you leaving here today—or tomorrow or whenever you plan on leaving? That I can't stand the thought that I won't be able to see you every day and have you to say good-night to every night?"

Uneasy advanced to full-out tension.

"That doesn't sound hypothetical," Kit said quietly, setting the coffee cup on the nightstand because she suddenly felt a little shaky and she didn't want it to show.

"What if it wasn't hypothetical?" he said every bit as quietly.

If it wasn't hypothetical then she had very mixed emotions about it. Emotions that ran the gamut from thrilled to terrified.

"I don't know," she said honestly.

"Would you be freaked out?"

"I'm the queen of freaking out when it comes to man-woman-relationship stuff, remember?"

"Are you freaking out right now?" he asked gently.

"A little bit."

Ad reached a hand to the spot just above her knee and squeezed. Even through the sheet it was comforting but it still didn't alleviate much of her stress about where this conversation was going.

"Don't freak out," he cajoled.

"I don't think I can help it."

He squeezed her knee again. "Try."

Oh, she was trying all right. She was trying very, very hard. But if he was saying what she thought he was saying, there wasn't much chance of her succeeding.

"What if again," he said gently, easing her back into what didn't seem like a game at all. "What if I said I'd do anything to get you up here? What if I said I'd personally move your business, set you up in whatever kind of place you need to be set up in, foot all the bills, and forevermore make sure that I took care of any complication that might arise in getting your cakes from here to anyone in the country who wanted them?"

"That's a lot."

"But worth it to me."

"Just so you could see me every day and say good-night to me every night?" Kit said, hedging again.

"And a little more," he answered cautiously.

"A little more?" she repeated.

"Okay, a lot more. Like, what if I wanted you in my life for the rest of it?"

Kit crossed the threshold into panic.

Clutching the sheet in a white-knuckled fist, she said, "What if you move me and my business to North-bridge—lock, stock and barrel—to have me in your life for the rest of it?"

"Yes. Are you totally freaking out now?"

"Totally," she said.

But even though it might have sounded as if she didn't completely mean it, she did. She was *totally* freaking out. And not because the idea he was so deli-cately attempting to warm her to wasn't appealing.

But because it *was* so appealing.

And because her mind was taking the idea and run-ning with it…

She honestly did like Northbridge. And Kira was here. Maybe they could be neighbors again and their friendship could go on the way it had been.

And she didn't even hate the thought of moving her business.

But more importantly what she was thinking was that even if none of that were true, Ad was here.

Ad, who was sitting there looking and smelling so wonderful, telling her he wanted her. That he wanted her so much he was willing to jump through hoops to have her.

And she wanted him, too. More than she'd ever wanted anyone else she'd been involved with. And not only because he was gorgeous and funny and fun and intelligent and warm and kind and thoughtful. And sexy. But also because he was a good man. A terrific man. An incredible man.

But no matter how fast her mind was racing with the positive side of this dilemma, everything it came up with about Ad was exactly why she knew she couldn't say yes to whatever it was he was proposing.

Sure, she could do what she was inclined to do at that moment. What she wanted to do—she could agree. But then what? Another run from another wedding? Another man left at the altar—and this one Ad?

Oh no, she couldn't do that. She couldn't forget those other two times when she'd agreed to join her life with the life of a man and then gotten cold feet at the last minute.

She couldn't forget the panic she'd felt—not unlike the panic she was feeling at that moment.

She couldn't forget the anxiety. The agony of realizing only when she was down to the wire that she couldn't go through with actually marrying them.

She couldn't forget the embarrassment of calling off the weddings.

And worst of all, she couldn't forget that she'd hurt and humiliated those other two men.

Because just the thought of Ad being on the other end

of that was unbearable to her. And no matter how incredible he was, she was just too afraid that she couldn't make it for the long haul. That she might end up doing to Ad—especially to Ad—what she'd done to Bert and Tim.

And she just couldn't do it to him.

"Talk to me, Kit," Ad said as if he were trying to draw her out of a coma.

Only then did she realize that she hadn't said anything since she'd confirmed that she was totally freaked out.

But the first thing she did when she emerged from her own thoughts wasn't to say anything to him.

The first thing she did was shake her head.

Then she said, "No," and the word seemed to reverberate off the walls of the studio apartment.

"I know," he reasoned. "It's an overwhelming proposition to think about when you factor in your business and the whole nine yards, but—"

"No. The fact that it's overwhelming isn't why I can't do it. I just can't do it."

"You wouldn't have to do hardly anything. I'd take care of everything."

"That's not what I mean. I just can't make another commitment I can't keep."

She hadn't thought that was harsh and yet Ad sat up a little straighter in response.

"Why couldn't you keep it?" he asked.

"I haven't been able to keep any of the others I've made—"

"Two of the others you've made. To two guys who were just wrong for you. But it isn't as if you've lived an entire life of broken commitments. You haven't. In fact, unless I've missed something, everything else you've ever committed yourself to you've accomplished."

But those two that she hadn't accomplished had been so important. Those two commitments she'd broken had hurt other people.

"Is it me?" Ad asked then. "Are you looking at me and seeing things you know you'd end up hating so much you'd do anything rather than have to put up with them?"

"No," she said yet again. "I'm looking at someone I can't bear the thought of hurting the way I hurt Bert and Tim."

"I'm willing to take the risk because I don't think that will happen."

And the reason he didn't think it would happen was because when it came to this he was naive. And because he was sure enough of himself to think that things would be different with him.

But Kit wasn't as sure of herself as he was of himself.

In fact she was so *un*sure that she knew she had to stick to the safest path. For the sake of them both.

"No, Ad. I can't do it. I'm serious."

"You're not serious, you're just scared. If you've fallen off roller skates both times you've tried to stand up on them, you're pretty leery about giving it a third shot. But it'll be okay, Kit."

"Bert and Tim thought it would be okay, too," she said in a fatalistic whisper. "But it wasn't. And it was my fault and I won't let it happen again."

The finality in her voice seemed to hang in the air.

"You don't mean that," Ad said after a moment of searching her eyes with his.

"I do mean it," she said firmly.

His brow beetled in disbelief. "Am I wrong? Am I the only one of us to feel like fate sent me the person who was perfect for me? The person I was destined for?"

"Maybe it's just a cruel trick of fate that that person is incapable of going the distance," she said more to herself than to him as a deep, deep sadness began to fill her.

"Incapable or just unwilling?" Ad asked.

Kit swallowed back the tears that began to swell in her throat.

"I just can't, Ad," she said forcefully, hating that the extent of the misery she felt sounded in her voice. "You deserve—"

"I deserve you."

She shook her head again. "No," she repeated once more.

Only this time it must have sunk in because he took his hand away and stood to look down at her with an expression that mingled anger and pain and frustration and disbelief all together.

"Two wrongs don't mean you can't *ever* get it right," he said.

"But two fiascoes are my limit."

"Then just don't let it be a fiasco."

As if it were that simple.

But Kit knew better. She knew what it was like to be gripped by such overwhelming terror about what she was getting into that she was willing to do anything, to suffer anything, to endure anything, to avoid it.

And she couldn't go through that again.

She couldn't put Ad at risk of being on the other side of it.

"I'm sorry," she said in a scant whisper.

"Not as sorry as I am."

Which was the point, and what she wanted to avoid on an even grander scale, Kit thought as he turned his back on her and crossed to the door.

It was just that once he was gone it was impossible for her to fathom that Ad—or anyone else—could feel worse than she did at that moment.

Chapter Ten

"No, no, no! You didn't really do that, did you?" Kira nearly shrieked three hours later Sunday morning after she'd picked up Kit and Kit's luggage, and driven her to Kira and Cutty's house.

The brunch was about to begin but on the drive from the apartment Kit hadn't been able to keep from crying and recounting to her friend what had happened earlier with Ad.

"Yes, I really did let him know there was no chance of a future with me. I had to," Kit insisted in response to Kira's rant.

"No, you *didn't* have to. You should have told Bert and Tim that you wouldn't marry them when they asked and because you didn't, you *had* to call off those weddings, but this isn't Tim or Bert. This is *Ad!*"

"Exactly—this is *Ad*. It was horrible enough that I hurt and embarrassed Tim and Bert. But that's what I kept thinking—*this is Ad*—and I couldn't risk that I might hurt him the same way."

They were in the nursery with the twins who were rummaging through their toy box while Kit and Kira sat on two miniature chairs at an equally miniature table with a pile of used tissues wadded up in front of Kit.

"I'm sorry, Kit," Kira said then. "I want to be supportive but this time you are so wrong."

"Ad is Cutty's best friend. He's the twins' godfather. He's *your* friend now. Do you really want him to be the *third* guy I leave hanging?"

"No, I don't. But I *really* don't think that would happen."

"Come on, Kira, you know me. You know what I did. Twice! You know that when it comes to a long-term commitment I just can't seem to make myself go through with it. Even when there's a church full of people waiting."

"I also know that Ad isn't Tim or Bert. And that you're different with him than you were with either of them. That everything I've seen between you and Ad is different."

This seemed to be the day for Kit to shake her head in denial because there she was, doing it again. "I agree that Ad isn't Tim or Bert, but you're wrong about me— I'm the same. That's the problem."

"You are not. With Tim and Bert it was as if you were just going through the motions. There was a part—a part of you that I knew—that you were holding back when you were with them. But that's not true when you're with Ad. You're more yourself than I've ever seen you with any other guy. It's like you've known each other forever. He walks into the room and you light up, you relax, you… Well, you're you. At your best. It's as if his just being there makes everything all right. It's the same for me with Cutty…" Kira seemed at a loss for how to describe it. "I don't know, it's like when we're together we're bigger than we are separately. We're stronger and more capable. We're…" Kira shrugged her shoulders. "This sounds hokey, but we're complete. And that's how you and Ad are. And that's not how you were with Tim or Bert."

Oddly enough—and Kit *did* think it was odd—she understood what her friend was saying. And Kira was right, she did feel stronger and more capable and, yes, more complete, when she was with Ad. Which was why rejecting him had been so hard on her and why she'd been a blubbering fool ever since.

But still that didn't convince her.

"The fact that things were so good with Ad—that he's such a good guy—are *why* I had to do what I did," Kit reiterated. "How awful would it be if fifteen minutes before I was set to marry him I started thinking about something I couldn't live with and I had to climb out another bathroom window? Not even you would go with me then."

"Okay, let's work with that," Kira said as if she were talking to one of the twins. "What's wrong with Ad that would make you climb out the bathroom window to keep from marrying him?"

Kit thought about that.

While she'd rejected Ad because she was afraid she would repeat her old patterns, she hadn't had any concrete reasons she could attribute to him and it made sense that she plug those kinds of details into the equation.

But right off the bat, it wasn't what was wrong with him that came to mind. It was what was right with him. He wasn't obsessed with everything being done a certain way—*his* way—like Bert had been, and he wasn't in need of constant strokes to his ego like Tim. But still, there had to be something negative. Nobody was perfect.

"There's that Northbridge Bruisers sports team he plays on—you know I hate sports," she said when she found herself trying to come up with something for too long.

"That's not a flaw in Ad. It's a hobby and Cutty does it, too, and it's no big deal, and you know it. I want to know what's wrong with him that would effect you every day, that your whole life would be influenced by like having to clean the bathroom with a toothbrush or having to tell someone what a star he was until you choke on the words."

Again Kit tried to think of something.

But whenever thoughts of Ad popped into her mind they only involved how terrific he looked, how sexy he was, how he made her laugh, how just the sound of his voice gave her warm flutters in the pit of her stomach, how his kisses could weaken her knees, how incredible their night of lovemaking had been.

Apparently Kira knew she was struggling to figure out what was wrong with Ad because she didn't wait any longer.

"I'll tell you what I think," she said. "And don't take this wrong, because Bert and Tim would have driven me crazy, too. But they both found people who can overlook the same things that you and I couldn't tolerate. And what that tells me is that finding flaws you couldn't live with in Bert and Tim was really just a warning that you didn't love them enough to marry them. To spend the rest of your life with them. It wasn't their flaws, Kit. Or the men themselves. Or you. It was that your feelings for them weren't deep enough. If they had been, the flaws wouldn't have mattered. And I think that your feelings for Ad are so deep that you can't even think of a flaw in him. Which makes for some pretty deep feelings, if you ask me."

"Or I'll think of a flaw as I walk down the aisle and I'll have to run the other way while everyone watches," Kit countered. "Assuming he was even asking me to marry him. It wasn't as if he actually said that."

"Honey?" Cutty called from downstairs just then. "We have company."

Kira craned her head in the direction of the door. "I'll be right there."

Then she turned back to Kit "Or maybe," she persisted, "you should just think about how you feel about Ad and if those feelings might be different than what you felt for Tim and Bert. And start with the fact that you care so much about Ad that you'd rather be as miserable as you are right now than risk hurting him."

Kira stood then and crossed to the twins, taking one of each of their hands. "Come on, girls," she said to them. "Aunt Kit needs some time to think and we need to go say hello to our guests." Then, tossing a stern frown at Kit, she said, "You and Ad helped me see what I should do when it came to Cutty. Now let me help you. Ad will be here any minute and I'm telling you to fix this with him. He's the one for you. Trust me even if you don't trust yourself."

And out Kira went with the toddlers.

But Kit didn't mind being left alone by then. Kira was right—she *did* need some time to think over what her friend had said because it was just sinking in that Kira might have a point.

Especially when it came to Kit's feelings for Ad.

What she felt for him was different from what she'd felt for both Tim and Bert. It was something that had gone through her mind in terms of the way Ad made her feel when he was kissing her, when he was touching her, last night when he'd made love to her. But for some reason that hadn't translated in her mind as having different feelings *for* him.

But now that she looked at it like that, it struck her that it was true.

Yes, she'd loved Tim and she'd loved Bert. But that love hadn't had the strength, the power, the depth of what she felt for Ad.

Being with them had been nice. But not as nice as being with Ad.

With Ad, no amount of time she spent with him

seemed like enough. No hour with him seemed too long.
No parting was welcome. And every minute she wasn't
with him seemed to drag. Seemed to be just something
to count until she could be with him again.

None of that had been true with either Bert or Tim.

It also occurred to her that even the way she felt at
that moment was an indication of a difference between the emotions Ad inspired in her and those from
her other two relationships. Yes, she'd suffered
hideous pangs of guilt over not going through with her
weddings to those other two men, but she'd also felt
relieved. And there was certainly none of that now.
Now relief was nowhere to be had and instead she was
devastated by a sadness and grief she could hardly
deal with.

So maybe Kira was right, Kit thought. Surely Ad
had to have flaws, no one was perfect. But her feelings
for him were so intense that she didn't notice flaws in
him any more than the women who Bert and Tim had
become involved with after her noticed anything wrong
with them.

And if that was the case, maybe she could actually
make it all the way down the aisle. All the way through
the rest of her life with Ad.

That thought brought with it a ray of hope, but also
another wave of concern.

Was she really going to move her entire business, her
entire life to a small town in *Montana?*

"There's a flaw," she muttered to herself, thinking of
how deeply imbedded were Ad's roots in this place and

the fact that she was the one who had to relocate not only herself, but the business she'd built from the ground up in Denver.

That idea was unsettling.

Until she considered the alternative and realized that this time around no flaw, no inconvenience, no sacrifice seemed too great.

Not when the alternative was to be anywhere, doing anything, without Ad.

Once her mind was made up, Kit left the nursery and locked herself in the upstairs bathroom to repair the damage a morning of crying had caused.

She dampened a washcloth with cool water and buried her face in it until the redness and puffiness around her eyes went away. Then she opened the medicine cabinet and availed herself of Kira's mascara and blush to do a little repair work.

She'd been too upset to bother much with her hair and had merely caught it in a ponytail. Now she took the rubber band out and finger-combed the unruly curls to fall loosely around her shoulders.

She wished she were wearing something sexier than the plain jeans and split V-neck T-shirt she had on, but there was nothing to be done about that. And even if there had been she wouldn't have changed because she was in a hurry to see Ad, to find out if turning down everything he'd offered this morning had made him decide she was too big a risk after all.

"I hope you didn't blow this for yourself," she informed her reflection, squaring her shoulders and leaving the bathroom to go downstairs.

Before the gifts were to be opened, the wedding brunch was being provided by Kira and Cutty's babysitter, Betty. So when Kit reached the lower level, she found the house full of people standing, sitting and leaning with plates in hand, enjoying the meal that was being served buffet-style in the dining room.

What she didn't see was Ad anywhere among them.

Surely he wouldn't miss this last wedding event, she reasoned as butterflies began to flutter in her stomach at the thought that he might stay away so he didn't have to see her.

But then she told herself that even if he hadn't come, she'd just borrow Kira's car and track him down. Because one way or another she wasn't going to let another hour pass without letting him know she'd been an idiot.

She exchanged only passing hellos with the other guests as she began to work her way through the house, scanning faces as she went. But Ad wasn't in the living room or out on the porch, he wasn't in the kitchen or in the backyard where the twins were entertaining two of the bridesmaids.

She did spy him in the dining room, though. From a distance since she'd come from the kitchen and he was leaning against the far wall near the doorway that led to the family room.

Talking to Amanda Barnes.

Kit would have preferred that he hadn't come at all

to finding him with the college secretary who had let him and everyone else know she wanted him.

But there they were and Kit couldn't help thinking that Amanda Barnes was right where Kit should have been—basking in the aquamarine gaze of those eyes that had no business being on the other woman.

"If you snooze, you lose."

Kit hadn't heard Kira come up from behind her and the whispered warning in her ear took her by surprise. Then Kira stepped to her side and it was clear she was watching the same thing Kit was.

"Again with Amanda Barnes?" Kit groused under her breath.

"I know. Betty invited her. I didn't even know she was coming or I would have warned you."

"I was going to talk to him," Kit informed her friend. "But I can't do it with *her* there."

Kira didn't respond to that. At least not to Kit. Instead, raising her voice, she said, "Amanda! I'm so glad you came," as she made a beeline for the secretary, said something Kit couldn't hear, and linked her arm through that of Amanda Barnes to lead her away from Ad.

Leaving him with a clear view of Kit.

But the minute he spotted her his expression went from placid to something much darker.

It was daunting and it made it more difficult for Kit to do what she wanted to do.

But not doing it wasn't an option, so she steeled herself with a deep breath and walked over to him.

"Hi," she said in a somewhat timid voice.

"Hi," he answered but without anything welcoming in his tone.

Still, Kit knew she had earned some coldness and she ignored it, plunging into the icy waters before she lost her nerve.

"Can we talk?"

"Depends."

She hadn't expected that. "On what?" she asked.

"On if you just want to say more of what you said this morning."

"Well, I do and I don't," she answered. "I mean, I want to talk about the same subject but things have changed."

His eyebrows shot up as if she'd roused his curiosity but for a moment he didn't say anything. He only studied her, leaving her to twist in the wind a bit.

Then he said, "Okay."

But she didn't want to talk to him there, in the middle of their friends' party, where anyone could hear.

"Can we go somewhere else?" she asked.

He shrugged one of those big shoulders negligently. "Where would you like to go?"

"How about the nursery?" she suggested, thinking that was neutral territory and wasn't likely to attract anyone else.

Ad pushed away from the wall. "I'll follow your lead."

Kit had the sense that that had a double meaning, that not only did she need to lead him to the nursery, she was going to have to take the lead once they got there, too.

But that was what she intended to do anyway, so she

took the first step by turning on her heels and heading upstairs with Ad following behind.

She'd been right about the nursery being free of party-goers. They had it to themselves when they got there. But once she was alone with Ad, with the nursery door closed, her anxiety level escalated tremendously.

So tremendously it made her fidgety and she grabbed a white teddy bear to hug while Ad leaned back against the door, crossed his arms over his chest, and merely watched her.

But now that the moment was at hand, she didn't know how to begin.

She only knew that the longer she let silence linger, the worse she felt, so she finally said, "You know, after I climbed out of the bathroom window before my last wedding my un-mother-in-law said I was a nut-job who didn't know a good thing when I had it. Since this morning I've been wondering if she was right."

"Second thoughts about her son?" Ad asked in a voice too deep to be as removed as he appeared to be.

"No. Second thoughts about you," she admitted.

He didn't remark. He just waited. Apparently for her to take more of the lead he'd warned her was all up to her.

So she blundered on.

"Kira gave me a talking-to and then she left me to think about it and I came up with a pretty big flaw in you."

One eyebrow arched in question.

"Your unbreakable ties to Northbridge and how anyone who wants to be with you has to either be a native or be willing to pick up everything and move here permanently. Some people could see that as pretty inflexible."

"It's been said before," he acknowledged. Then he pointed his chin at one of the nursery's windows. "But if you're going to climb out to get away from it you shouldn't have picked the second floor."

"I don't need to climb out to get away from it. I don't want to get away from it at all. I was just saying that you aren't flawless."

He almost cracked a smile. "Who said I was?"

"Well, me, actually. When I was trying to tell Kira what there was about you that might send me running a third time."

"But then she left you to think about it and you came up with a reason to bail—is that what you wanted to tell me?"

"No. I wanted to tell you that even though I thought of a reason to bail—a pretty big flaw, by the way—it still didn't freak me out. Even though I admit that I did freak out this morning thinking about how I might freak out in the future."

She wasn't sure she was making any sense at all. But just in case he'd understood any of that, she added, "And I'm thinking that there's a good chance that I won't freak out down the road, either."

Trying for more coherence, Kit went on to explain Kira's theory that the depth of her feelings made the difference between those last two relationships and what she had with Ad, explaining all she'd worked out for herself after talking to her friend.

Ad listened and watched her closely as she went through the whole thing. And although he didn't comment, she thought that his expression, his whole body, seemed to be relaxing more as she went along.

"So playing *what if,*" she said when she'd finished, mimicking his earlier approach. "What if I said I just might be willing to let you move my business and me up here? What would you say?"

"I'd say I want you to marry me," he said as if he was concerned that she didn't intend to go that far.

"Even with my track record?"

"Did it get worse since this morning?"

That made her smile and relax a little herself. "I told you, two fiascoes are my limit."

"Then if you say you'll marry me, you'll have to do it."

"Yes, I guess I will."

"Yes, you'll marry me? Or, yes, you'll have to marry me if you say you will?" he asked for clarification.

But Kit didn't give in. Instead she said, "Are you sure you want to take the chance on me? That you won't be prostrate with worry that at any moment I might climb out a window and disappear?"

"Why would you climb out a window and disappear on Mr. Flawless?" he said with a genuine smile beginning at the corners of his mouth.

"I'm just saying that with my history—"

"I believe that, if you tell me you'll marry me, you will," he said confidently, coming to stand in front of her then.

"I believe," he continued once he got there, "that you

had to call off those other two weddings because you were destined to wait for me. And all they're going to be is a funny story we tell our great-grandchildren about how great-grandma ditched a couple of other guys before I swept her off her feet."

Ad took the teddy bear out of her hands, tossed it into the toy box and put her arms around his waist so he could do the same to her to close the gap between them.

"I'm the guy for you," he said then. "Those others were only posers and you were smart enough to see through them."

"But still you'll worry until the *I-do's* are said," she said, recalling what she'd overheard him tell Cutty before the wedding.

But if that was still true, he didn't confess to it. Instead, sounding as if he wasn't concerned in the slightest, he said, "I think you'll worry more than I will."

Then he bent down to kiss her, softly, chastely. His warm lips were supple and sweet on hers, and as lazy as if they had a lifetime to spend there.

And when he stopped kissing her, he looked intently into her eyes and, in a quiet voice, said, "Does this mean you're saying you *will* marry me?"

"If you're brave enough to take the chance, so am I," Kit said.

"I'm brave enough."

"Then let's give it a try."

"Let's give it a try," Ad agreed.

He kissed her with a much more passionate kiss that pressed her head back into his waiting hand and made her melt against him as Kit lost herself to him, to that kiss, to all those things only he could awaken in her.

And all the while she was holding hard to the hope that the third time really would be the charm.

Epilogue

"Okay, once more," Ad said into the dark of the studio apartment. "Do you, Kit MacIntyre take this man to be your lawfully wedded husband?"

Kit was lying in his arms, using his muscular chest as a pillow. "I do," she said, smiling against the warmth of his skin. "I do, I do, I do."

"Then I *now*—"

"*Again*—" Kit amended.

"—pronounce us husband and wife. And I may kiss the bride."

Ad did exactly that, kissing the top of her head to denote the end of the little game he'd been playing since their wedding earlier that evening.

But Kit didn't mind. In the whirlwind three weeks since she'd said she would marry him and they'd closed

Kit's Cakes in Denver, moved her to Northbridge and set the wheels into motion to reestablish her business, she'd suffered a low-grade tension as she'd continued to worry that, at the last minute, she might still flip out and run before she made it to the altar with Ad.

Now that they'd had their small, quiet garden ceremony and reception in Kira's and Cutty's backyard and returned to spend their wedding night in the studio apartment where it had all started for them—even though they were sharing the larger apartment next door as their home—and now that their marriage was consummated, every vestige of Kit's tension was gone. So Ad could play whatever game he wanted.

"You know, when you told me about climbing out the bathroom window fifteen minutes before that second wedding of yours you said you got down to the wire because you were trying so hard to go through with it," Ad said then, running his fingertips up and down her arm.

"Uh-huh," Kit confirmed, tracing his pectorals with some featherlight strokes of her own.

"So I keep wondering if you went all the way through this wedding just to save face and you're planning to dump me tomorrow in a late-stage freak-out."

She could tell by the lazily playful note in his voice that he was teasing her. "You caught me—a couple more rolls in the hay and I'm out of here."

He laughed and squeezed her tight. "Only a couple more? I'm Mr. Flawless and all I get is a *couple* more?"

Kit tilted her chin to look at him. "Mr. Flawless?" she repeated facetiously. "Is that the same guy who leaves his dirty socks on the floor and drinks out of the milk container and litters the butter with toast crumbs? That Mr. Flawless?"

Ad craned his head forward enough to kiss her lips— a kiss she was familiar with as the signal that things were stirring in him again despite the fact that they'd already made love twice since leaving their reception.

A kiss that lasted awhile before he ended it and said, "Are you telling me now that I *do* have flaws?"

"One or two."

"Enough flaws to make you flee?"

He was very proud of his attempt at alliteration because he was grinning down at her.

Kit was feeling a few stirrings of her own and decided to help things along by pressing a kiss against his taut male nib and then flicking the tip of her tongue against it before she said, "No. Not enough flaws to make me flee. Just flaws I'm going to train you out of."

"Ooh, I like the sound of that," he said lasciviously, as if she'd promised something very sexy.

Kit laughed and then moaned a little as he reached a big hand to one of her breasts and began the magic only he could work there.

"Think I can persuade you to stick around a little longer if I bow to your will?" he asked as the persuasion of that hand and the thigh he raised between her legs made her will weaken considerably.

"Maybe," she said, trailing her own hand down his flat belly to that part of him that could drive her to the brink of madness.

The brink of madness she knew just how to drive him to, too, as she enclosed that long, hard staff in her grip and made him groan even louder than she had.

He didn't ask any more questions for the time being. Instead he captured her mouth with his again as a passion that seemed always just below the surface came to life and swept them away.

And before Kit even thought about it, limbs were entwined. Hands were seeking and finding, teasing and tormenting and elevating desire to greater and greater heights. Heights that left neither of them able to contain themselves.

Bodies came together, joining in a perfect union of flesh and spirit to soar to the pinnacle of pleasure. A pleasure that they'd both come to know well in the brief time they'd been together.

And then slowly that pleasure spent itself and eased them back to the reality of lying in each other's arms again, exhausted, replete, fulfilled once more.

Another moment passed as they remained bathed in that blissful afterglow and then, in a raspy voice that echoed with emotion, Ad said, "Have I told you recently how much I love you?"

Kit buried her face in his neck. "I know you love me enough to risk being my third try at making it all the way through a wedding of my own," she said.

"I love you even more than that. I love you so much I would have been your third and fourth and fifth— you're *hundredth* try, if that's how many it took to get you down the aisle to me."

"Well, it didn't take that many because I love you, too," she said then. "That's really why we made it."

"I know. That's why we'll make it forever," he whispered as if he were too weary to summon more.

But Kit didn't need more.

As she laid in Ad's arms and began to give herself over to sleep, too, she knew that she had everything she needed right there, with him.

And now that she did, she didn't have a single doubt, a single qualm, a single regret.

Not when she knew that she'd finally, truly, found her heart's desire. Not when she knew that the commitment she'd made to Ad was as complete as he made her feel.

Because flaws or no flaws, what she felt for him was unlike anything she'd ever felt before.

And although she still regretted hurting those other two men and causing the chaos she'd caused, she honestly believed that those other two times had only been the near misses that had led her to this man.

This man who she knew she would never run from.

This man who she loved, flaws and all.

* * * * *

Look for the next book in
Victoria Pade's Northbridge Nuptials Miniseries,
HAVING THE BACHELOR'S BABY,
in January 2005!

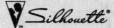

SPECIAL EDITION™

Coming in September 2004
from beloved author

ALLISON LEIGH

Home on the Ranch

(Silhouette Special Edition #1633)

When his daughter suffered a riding
accident, reclusive rancher Cage Buchanan
vowed to do anything to mend his daughter's
broken body and spirit. Even if that promise
meant hiring his enemy's daughter, Belle Day.
And though Cage thought Belle was the last
person he needed in his life, she drew him
like a moth to a flame....

Available at your favorite retail outlet.

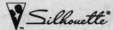

SPECIAL EDITION™

The Baby They Both Loved

by

NIKKI BENJAMIN

(Silhouette Special Edition #1635)

The lure of Simon Gilmore's
masculine strength was almost more
than Kit Davenport could resist.
But as long as he had the right to
take her adopted baby—*his* son—
away from her, he was the enemy....

Wasn't he?

*Available September 2004
at your favorite retail outlet.*

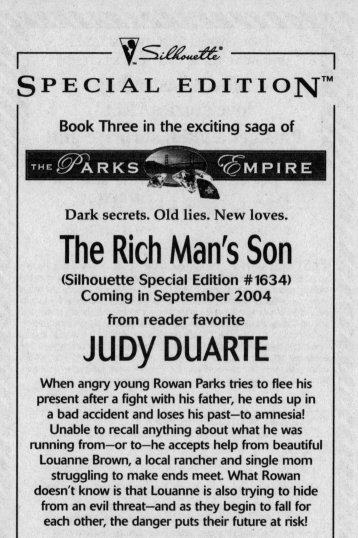

Silhouette®

SPECIAL EDITION™

Book Three in the exciting saga of

THE PARKS EMPIRE

Dark secrets. Old lies. New loves.

The Rich Man's Son

(Silhouette Special Edition #1634)
Coming in September 2004

from reader favorite

JUDY DUARTE

When angry young Rowan Parks tries to flee his
present after a fight with his father, he ends up in
a bad accident and loses his past—to amnesia!
Unable to recall anything about what he was
running from—or to—he accepts help from beautiful
Louanne Brown, a local rancher and single mom
struggling to make ends meet. What Rowan
doesn't know is that Louanne is also trying to hide
from an evil threat—and as they begin to fall for
each other, the danger puts their future at risk!

Available at your favorite retail outlet.

If you enjoyed what you just read,
then we've got an offer you can't resist!

Take 2 bestselling love stories FREE!

Plus get a FREE surprise gift!

Clip this page and mail it to Silhouette Reader Service™

IN U.S.A.
3010 Walden Ave.
P.O. Box 1867
Buffalo, N.Y. 14240-1867

IN CANADA
P.O. Box 609
Fort Erie, Ontario
L2A 5X3

YES! Please send me 2 free Silhouette Special Edition® novels and my free surprise gift. After receiving them, if I don't wish to receive anymore, I can return the shipping statement marked cancel. If I don't cancel, I will receive 6 brand-new novels every month, before they're available in stores! In the U.S.A., bill me at the bargain price of $4.24 plus 25¢ shipping and handling per book and applicable sales tax, if any*. In Canada, bill me at the bargain price of $4.99 plus 25¢ shipping and handling per book and applicable taxes**. That's the complete price and a savings of at least 10% off the cover prices—what a great deal! I understand that accepting the 2 free books and gift places me under no obligation ever to buy any books. I can always return a shipment and cancel at any time. Even if I never buy another book from Silhouette, the 2 free books and gift are mine to keep forever.

235 SDN DZ9D
335 SDN DZ9E

Name	(PLEASE PRINT)	
Address	Apt.#	
City	State/Prov.	Zip/Postal Code

Not valid to current Silhouette Special Edition® subscribers.

Want to try two free books from another series?
Call 1-800-873-8635 or visit www.morefreebooks.com.

* Terms and prices subject to change without notice. Sales tax applicable in N.Y.
** Canadian residents will be charged applicable provincial taxes and GST.
 All orders subject to approval. Offer limited to one per household.
 ® are registered trademarks owned and used by the trademark owner and or its licensee.

SPED04R   ©2004 Harlequin Enterprises Limited

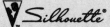

SPECIAL EDITION™

A Texas Tale

by

JUDITH LYONS

(Silhouette Special Edition #1637)

Crissy Albreit was a bona fide risk taker
as part of the daredevil troupe the
Alpine Angels. But Tate McCade was
offering a risk even Crissy wasn't sure
she wanted to take: move to Texas and
run the ranch her good-for-nothing
father left behind after his death. Crissy
long ago said goodbye to her past.
Now this McCade guy came bearing
a key to it? And maybe even one to
her future as well....

*Available September 2004
at your favorite retail outlet.*

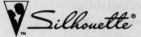

COMING NEXT MONTH

#1633 HOME ON THE RANCH—Allison Leigh
Men of the Double S
Rancher Cage Buchanan would do anything to help his child—
even if it meant enlisting the aid of his enemy's daughter.
Beautiful Belle Day could no more ignore Cage's plea for help
than she could deny the passion that smoldered between them.
But could a long-buried secret undermine the happiness they'd
found in each other's arms?

#1634 THE RICH MAN'S SON—Judy Duarte
The Parks Empire
After prodigal heir Rowan Parks suffered a motorcycle accident,
single mom Luanne Brown took him in and tended to his wounds.
Bridled emotion soon led to unleashed love, but there was one
hitch: he couldn't remember his past—and she couldn't forget
hers….

#1635 THE BABY THEY BOTH LOVED—Nikki Benjamin
When writer Simon Gilmore discovered a son he never knew
was his, he had to fight the child's legal guardian, green-eyed
waitress Kit Davenport, for custody. Initially enemies, soon
Simon and Kit started to see each other in a new light. Would
the baby they both loved lead to one loving family?

#1636 A FATHER'S SACRIFICE—Karen Sandler
After years of battling his darkest demons, Jameson O'Connell
discovered that Nina Russo had mothered his chid. The world-
weary town outcast never forgot the passionate night that they
shared and was determined to be a father to his son…but could
his years of excruciating personal sacrifice finally earn him the
love of his life?

#1637 A TEXAS TALE—Judith Lyons
Rancher Tate McCade's mission was to get Crissy Albreit back
to the ranch her father wanted her to have. Not only did Tate's
brown-eyed assurance tempt Crissy back to the ranch she so
despised, but pretty soon he had her tempted into something
more…to be in his arms forever.

#1638 HER KIND OF COWBOY—Pat Warren
Jesse Calder had left Abby Martin with a promise to return…
but that had been five years ago. Now, the lies between them
may be more than Abby can forgive—even with the spark still
burning. Especially since this single mom is guarding a secret of
her own: a little girl with eyes an all-too-familiar shade of Calder
blue…